THE
FEAR
OF
SOMEDAY

BY JENNIE ENDICOTT

Dorrance Publishing Co
585 Alpha Drive
Pittsburgh, PA 15238
Visit our website at *www.dorrancebookstore.com*

ISBN: 979-8-89027-029-0
eISBN: 979-8-89027-527-1

The Fear of Someday

CHAPTER 1

For the longest time, someday was just a dream or a thought in my mind. But suddenly someday is almost here and I'm terrified. I need to escape. I'm exhausted from so much hurt and disappointment in my life, mostly brought on by myself. I've allowed the people in my life to control and dictate what was going to be. Regardless of knowing it was wrong. Unfortunately, my own decisions made at a young age landed me in a very bad place.

But today is different. Today there may be hope for a better life. All these years of planning an escape have finally become real. And I have never been so scared in my life! My name is Jenna Graham, and I'm going to disappear, hopefully without a trace. Never to be seen or heard from again. A new life for me, leaving everything I've ever known behind. My husband James of twenty years, also my high school sweetheart, has been the biggest source of my pain and disappointment. I was a freshman in high school and he was a senior when we met. I was attracted to his smile at first, his perfect straight white teeth, and a really big smile. He's tall and slim with light brown eyes. To me he hasn't aged much. Although, I don't see him the same as I once did. Everything in our marriage has been a lie. On the outside everyone thinks we have the perfect marriage, but behind closed doors, it's ugly to say the least. He doesn't allow me to go anywhere without him. I have no friends except Bert and I no longer see my family. James never did care for any of my family, and to be honest neither did I. That's a story for another day, but right now in this moment, my journey will begin.

Bert, who is my only friend, is also my keeper hired by James and has been for several years. In the beginning, James allowed me to see my friends, but as time went on it all changed. He became violent and controlling. I'm barely allowed to leave the house, not even supervised by Bert. James travels a lot so I would get the occasional reprieve from being his prisoner. But Bert was always there. Making sure I was being the dutiful wife. James did give me money on occasion to shop for myself, and every chance I got, I bought a little something I would need should my escape ever come to fruition. The treasure chest as I called it, hidden in the floor in the room where I spent so many hours alone. Here, I cried myself to sleep wondering how this became my life. Over time, I think Bert felt sorry for me. If James would give me a beating, or a lesson as he would call it, Bert would come to check on me. I began to trust him and feel thankful that I had him. Sometimes he stayed with me for hours just talking about insignificant things. I'm only beginning to realize how important he is to me.

James and I had one son soon after we married, James Jr., and we called him Junior for short. He's nineteen now and away at college. He is an exact replica of his father. He has no resemblance of me whatsoever. It's hard to believe how fast time has gone by. Unfortunately, my relationship with him isn't what I had envisioned. Like every pregnant mother, you dream of what your life with your child is going to be like. You imagine kisses and cuddles and a love far beyond anything else. Sadly, my son treats me like his father does. He's a rich, spoiled brat who's been raised primarily by his father and his nanny Lola. To him, I'm insignificant just as his father taught him. He's disrespectful and rarely comes to see me. When he does it's generally a brief visit, almost like he feels guilty or obligated. The sincere, soft moments are rare, but I take those moments and hold them close to my heart. Don't get me wrong, I love my son. I'll always love my son. But I can't trust him not to tell his father about the escape. He's extremely loyal to him. Even though James is a bastard, I had hoped to win the heart of my son, but it just didn't happen. I spent so many hours crying over him. So many that now I just feel broken and indifferent. But somehow I survived the grief. I think in part because I knew in my heart that someday an opportunity to escape this prison would come. I didn't know how or when but that it just had to happen. Hope is how I survived.

Bert has been helping me behind James's back. He's been a loyal friend to James, but he has developed feelings for me and I for him. Not in a romantic sort of way but more like a father/daughter sort of way. Bert is probably fifteen years older than James and me. He's never disclosed his real age to me, not that it matters. He told me that he spent quite a few years as a Navy seal and then worked for the witness protection program. He's about 6'3" and is a pretty large guy, as in super fit for his age. His hair is thick and dark with gray starting to take over. He has big blueish-green beautiful eyes. James met him at a gun show many years ago. I can only assume that James is paying him well in order for him to give up his former career choices.

Bert told me that James is in a romantic relationship with Lola, but I already knew. I can see it when they are together. If she could only see her future, she wouldn't be so foolish. I'm not even mad, I simply feel sorry for her. For me though, it means James comes to me in the night less and less. I'm thankful for that. She's young, blond and beautiful, much like I used to be. Now my hair is turning a darker blond with an occasional gray hair presenting itself to remind me that I'm getting older. I'm also starting to see some fine lines appearing around my big brown eyes. I guess I should be thankful that I don't look many years older than I actually am. At 35 I look pretty good. I've maintained a healthy weight thanks to my limited food intake. James keeps me at 1200 calories a day to ensure he doesn't have a fat wife. It's for my own good, he says. One day I will never be hungry, a promise I am making to myself. And definitely one I intend to keep.

CHAPTER 2

Yes, there's no question, panic has definitely set in. I am so afraid that James is going find out about our plan and that Bert helped me. For the life of me, I'll never be able to understand how Bert can be associated with a man like James, but here we are. He's the head of security for all of James's affairs to include me. But last night Bert shared some disturbing news. He informed me that James asked him to make me disappear, as in kill me. I don't know why, but my heart is broken. No matter how horrible James is, he is still my husband. My husband that wants me dead. I'm assuming so he can have a life with Lola. If he legally divorces me, I would get half of everything and he's never going to let that happen.

Thankfully Bert has taken pity on me and developed a plan to help me escape, a plan to start a new life. So he says anyway. I guess that remains to be seen. For all I know, he's just saying that so I will willingly go with him only to be met with my demise. Time will tell.

For me, the escape plan has become my hope, my reality, my lifeline. I'm choosing to believe Bert has good intentions. As of now, I have no idea where I'm going, only that Bert has been tasked with getting rid of me. He said James wants it to happen sometime in the next few weeks. He'll be out of town on a business trip providing him with a solid alibi. After that, the only information Bert has shared is that I can never come back and that I'll be safe. I have no choice but to trust him and hope he won't betray me.

Since learning of the plot to end my life, I've been taking advantage of the time I spend alone. Every chance I get, I put a little something back that I may need when I finally get a place of my own. Things like dish towels, washcloths, and a few bedding items. I even have a new set of silverware. A tiny bud vase that I really like too. But I'm not going to lie. Going through my personal things has been painful. I'm struggling to understand how this became my life. How did I become a prisoner in my own home? To help me get through this madness, I started pretending that these things I've collected are my treasures. Silly I know, but it adds some excitement to what is in reality a nightmare.

Bert did tell that me that I can't take much so I'll make sure to take the necessities to include some clothing, personal items, a few of my new things and a few cherished items although there aren't many of those. I'm assuming so James doesn't notice the missing items and cause unnecessary suspicion. I was instructed no pictures or personal identification of any kind. Bert provided me with a matching set of leather bags. The set includes a large backpack, a rolling duffle and a cross body bag, all in black. Not really my color, but it's what he provided. So for now it just has to work. Maybe some time I'll find something that's a little more me. Bert said nothing outside of those bags can be taken. Everything must be in my bags, no ancillary items. Since James will be out of town for the next few days, I can spend a little more time on my selections. I will definitely have to be careful as I'm not sure if Lola is going with James or if she'll be staying here. My hope is that she's going. I'll be able to move around a little more freely, sort of. I mean there are security guards on the premises at all times. Hence the reason I've never been able to run. Although, I tried once many years ago. James found me not long after I left and he beat me to near death. Bad enough that I spent a whole week in the hospital. Since James's property runs for many, many miles, there was no where to run to and no place to hide. Just acres and acres of lonely roads. He told me if I ever tried to leave again, there wouldn't be a need for medical assistance. Meaning the end of my life. I took him seriously and never tried again. I've convinced myself that if I just stay quiet, things aren't so bad. There will always be others in far worse situations than my own. I have to always see the good or what is the point of having any life at all?

Today is Saturday and I'm going to spend the day looking and sorting through my belongings, or my treasures. One might think treasures consist of diamonds, silver and gold, but for me, a treasure is simply something I might need when I finally have a place of my own. Kitchen towels and cooking utensils are something I've only dreamed about. James has a cook as well so I've never had a kitchen of my own. I've never cooked a meal for my son. I've never been a real wife or mother. But I dream and ponder about it all the time. I would love to have a real marriage with a house, kids and a dog.

We live in a mansion built by James's father. At least it feels like a mansion, and I never really thought about what the size requirements are for a mansion. I think Bert told me it's about 7000 square feet. So it's a very large house. It is decorated in very dark colors and has always been such a cold, unloving place. In my dreams of having a place of my own, I see it so differently. I picture it to be small in size with a bright and airy feel. I see white walls and doors, lots of windows and decorated in a white and cream color alette and maybe a touch of blue and green. I'll have a lightly fragranced candle burning, maybe something floral like lavender. The thought of this has my heart doing leaps. I'll go to church on Sunday, maybe work as a cook in a restaurant, and plant lots of flowers. Sometimes the possibility of that life is the only thing that has helped me to survive. I patiently waited for this day to come. I prayed and prayed for this day to come. It took a little longer than I had imagined, but it is going to happen. It has to. I'm running out of steam and the days seem to be getting longer and longer. I sleep a lot to help pass the time, but I'm looking forward to better days.

Chapter 3

Someday is here. Bert told me tonight is the night. My heart is pounding so hard and loud that I'm afraid someone is going to hear it. What if he catches us? How will Bert prove that I'm actually dead to James? Is Bert really going to spare my life? So many thoughts and emotions right now. Bert just left to take James and Lola to the airport. That answers the question about her staying here. Thank goodness she is going with James. One less thing to worry about for sure. Bert said when he gets back from dropping them off, we'll put the plan in motion.

It felt like Bert was gone forever but it was only a few hours. My sense of time doesn't seem to exist anymore. It kind of all runs together as of late. My heart is pounding like never before and I am so scared. Can fear kill a person? In this moment I'm thinking yes and that I might actually have a heart attack. Breathe, I keep telling myself. In….out….in…out. Oh god. Bert is coming to my room. Is he going to hurt me or help me? I almost collapsed right then and there. In the next moment, he walked in my room. He could see the fear I was feeling and hugged me. He said it's all going to be alright. I promise. For a brief moment I believed him. I am now wondering how he will get my bags out of here without being caught on camera. And James will want proof that the job is done no doubt. Bert hasn't mentioned how this is going to happen and I haven't asked. Trust. It's all I have right now. But if he's really going to take my life, I hope it's fast. Lord knows I have had enough sadness and suffering to last two lifetimes.

Just as my thoughts had taken over, Bert reached up and turned the camera off in my room. He said the rest have already been turned off, further explaining his reason to James will be that he didn't want any evidence to ever arise relating to my disappearance. That made sense to me, and James trusts him so he'll believe whatever Bert tells him. Although in thinking about this, there is no one to report me missing, so I'm guessing he told James he's covering his tracks just in case.

Bert carried my bags out to his blue Ford Explorer. He told me to wait in my room and he'd be back shortly. I paused and took one last look around the room that I spent so many lonely hours. Wondering to myself if I would miss it. Only because it's all I've known for so long. Tears ran down my cheek as I stood there afraid. Hoping I'm truly going to have a better life. I've lived in Texas all my life. I've never been to a beach, a lake, camping, amusement parks or anywhere for that matter. These are places I have only dreamed about. Will my new life let me experience the beauty I've seen on TV? I certainly hope so.

Bert returned to my room and asked me if I was ready. I replied with a fearful yes. He took my hand and led me from my room. To where I don't know yet. Like an obedient child, I simply held his hand and followed. I got in his SUV and sat quietly as we pulled out of the long, long winding driveway. I had one last quick glimpse of the mansion and swore I would wipe this place from my memory, although I know that will be easier said than done. The image in the rear-view mirror was not a pleasant one for sure. I did make a promise to myself to find happiness in whatever life I was going to live. Freedom will be the ultimate accomplishment. My own independence. What is this even going to feel like?

Once we got on the road, it was getting dark. I saw Bert turn his phone off. I've never had my own phone, but I guess I never really needed one. I asked him why he turned it off.

"It's best if no one can track us," he replied in a faint almost weak, exhausted voice. I realized in that moment this must be hard for him too. After all, pretending to plan my murder as directed by James and fine-tuning every detail of my escape, wow! I never thought about the time and effort he must have put into saving my life. I could definitely see the worry on his face. And then panic set in once again. Oh good grief! Now I'm back to questioning his intent. Is he or is he not going to kill me? As my thoughts we're wondering off, he started to speak, and I nearly jumped out of my own skin. I was startled just by him speaking. What is wrong with me?

"Relax and try to get some rest," he said. "We have a very long drive over the next few days. We're taking the roads less traveled."

"That's it? That's all I get?" I replied. "It's my life on the line and I have a right to know the plan."

Once again, he told me to rest and that we would talk about the plan once we've stopped for a break. Humph! Angry, I rolled over and covered up with the blanket I packed. I no sooner rolled over and I was out.

Chapter 4

Iwoke up and looked out the window. The sun was coming up. A beautiful sunrise actually. I just stared for a moment and then looked over to Bert to see if he was awake. Only Bert wasn't there. I looked around and realized we were stopped in some secluded wooded place. I started searching around the SUV for a weapon. I didn't find one. If Bert is going to kill me, it won't be without a fight that's for sure! I jumped out of the car and grabbed the biggest rock I could find. Just then he appeared. My heart racing once again, I started running with the rock. Stupid idea! I dropped it on my big toe and fell. I can hear Bert right behind me laughing. I rolled over and realized I had succumbed to my own death without a fight. I was instantly ashamed of myself. Bert, still laughing, reached out a hand to help me up.

"What are you doing?" he asked.

"I thought you were going to kill me," I said. "You were gone when I woke up. What was I supposed to think?"

"Good grief, woman, I had to piss," he replied. "I pulled over to relieve myself and didn't want to wake you. Haven't we been over this multiple times? I'm not going to hurt you." He started laughing.

Slightly embarrassed, I got up with my injured toe and pride and limped back to his SUV. "I'm sorry," I told him. "I've just been so scared for so long that my mind wanders off a bit sometimes. But I don't appreciate you laughing at me. You have no idea what it's been like on this emotional roller coaster."

Bert just nodded as if he understood and apologized for laughing. "I'll wake you the next time I need to piss," he said with a big grin. We got back in the SUV and started driving again.

A few hours later, we stopped at a little dive restaurant in the middle of nowhere. I'm starving and I have to pee so I didn't much care where we stopped. I was so rattled at the last stop I forgot to go to the bathroom. To say I've been uncomfortable for the last few hours is definitely an understatement! There aren't many roadside rests when you take the roads less traveled, that's for certain. We were lucky to find a gas station earlier, but it didn't have public restrooms. Thankfully we found this place just in time. I'm pretty sure I was on the verge of a ruptured bladder.

We were seated and ordered our food and drinks. There was silence between us for a few minutes, and then I just couldn't be silent any longer. I had to ask.

"Where are we, Bert, and where are you taking me? I need to know, I deserve to know."

He looked as if he'd seen a ghost and simply sat there.

"I'm waiting for an answer."

"I'm sorry," he said. "I know you deserve answers. God knows you deserve so much more. I just really didn't want our journey to turn south before we get there."

"What do you mean?" I asked. "I'm confused."

Bert simply replied, "Can we please just enjoy our meal and I promise answers when we get on the road. This is not the time or place for this conversation."

We were back to sitting in silence. Luckily not for too long because our food came. I am so hungry. I ordered a cheeseburger with French fries and a strawberry milkshake. Bert ordered two cheeseburgers, a large fry and a Coke. I'm pretty sure he was starving too. He inhaled his first burger. Done before I had three bites of mine.

I enjoyed being out and having lunch with another human. I almost felt giddy. Although I'm not sure why. Maybe just knowing I never have to go back. I still can't believe this is really happening. Somebody pinch me please!

We both used the bathroom again on the way out and then ordered coffees to go. The smell of fresh brewed coffee is amazing! I can't wait to have a drink! Hopefully our conversation goes well. Judging by his response, I think I'm in for some unpleasant news. Luckily, I'm not feeling any fear today, just some anxiety. But coffee and conversation can be a good thing. I'm going to work really hard at being positive.

CHAPTER 5

We buckled our seatbelts and I adjusted my seat back to an upright position. I then wrapped my legs in the blanket to hopefully take the chill away. Now I'm ready for the conversation with Bert. At least I think I am.

I could see in his eyes that he is troubled by what he's going to tell me. "I'm just going to spit it out," he blurted. "There's no sugarcoating what has to be said. But first I'm going to apologize and tell you who I really am." I must have a fearful look again because he grabbed my hand and told me once more that it's all going to be okay.

Then he began.

"My real name is Mac Lewis. I'm an undercover agent for the DEA. Everything you know about me is false. Bert was a character created for me to go deep under cover. Created to help take down one of the biggest drug lords in Texas. I'm so sorry to have to be the one to tell you, James is a big-time drug dealer." He could see my face turn to hurt, big crocodile tears filling my eyes. *She clearly didn't know. And now I'm just another disappointment to her. I've lied to her for years and I can see the look of hurt, disbelief and maybe a bit of anger.*

As he was apologizing yet again, I couldn't stop the tears no matter how hard I tried. I realized in that moment he could have saved me a long time ago. How could he sit back and watch all the years of pain, starvation and abuse I have endured. He's an officer of the law, right? How, I just don't understand. My sobs turned to a river of tears that just wouldn't stop. He reached for my hand again to comfort me, but I pulled away. Sadness and anger have taken over, and I feel like someone just ripped my heart out. I feel physically sick.

"Pull over," I told him. "Now!"

Bert, Mac whoever this bastard is, pulled over as he was told. He stayed quiet allowing me to process what he just told me. I hurriedly got out of his SUV and threw up my lunch. My mind is racing. Do I want to run? I'm in the middle of nowhere. Where would I go if I do run? If what he says is true, I'll never be free. The tears just keep coming. I must have sat on my knees for the better part of two hours. I cried until I had nothing left. I pulled myself together and walked back to his SUV. I reached into my bag for a cold wet face wipe and began to clean myself up.

We got back on the road, and I asked him to please finish what he had to say.

"Are you sure?" he asked.

"Yes, most definitely. I need to know what's going to happen to me."

Bert started to talk again as I was making yet another promise to myself to hold it together. At least until I'm alone and can have my breakdown in private.

He began to speak. "James is a very bad person, far beyond what you already know or can even imagine. He's hidden so much from you. It's been tough for law enforcement to bring him in for an arrest. He's really smart with his business, and his people that work for him are extremely loyal. No one has been able to break any of them into talking. And not for lack of trying. All of the people who worked for him and tried to leave seem to have disappeared. He rules with fear, as you already know. His people are terrified of him and rightfully so. I arrested one of his men several years ago, and he took his own life while in custody. He left a note stating it was easier to take his own life rather than face the big boss. He said he knew he was a walking dead man and couldn't bear the thought of it. In his suicide letter, he further stated that at least this way it would be quick and on his terms. He wished us luck in our endeavors to take him down, but he was careful even in his death to not use James's name for fear they would go after his family. So once again we had nothing. Back to square one."

"So why now?" I asked. "Do you really have enough to put him away this time? Why should I trust you? You let him lock me in a room like an animal, starve me for days at a time and beat me unconscious. What human can do that? Right now I don't think you're any better than he is." I started to cry again and now I'm shaking. *Please hold it together*, I keep telling myself. But I just couldn't convince myself that I was going to be okay. They don't know him like I do. He'll keep looking for me, and if that's the case, no one involved with me is safe.

"If I could have done anything different to save you sooner, I promise I would have. You have no idea how hard this has been on me. Nothing, I know, compared to what you have endured. But now we have him for the hit on your life, and it's a solid case, I promise. I have texts from him and Lola asking me to take care of it sooner rather than later. It's not a coincidence that she's been a nanny to your son. It's all been part of a bigger plan. She comes from a long line of cartel family including her dad and brother. They met on a massive drug deal. Her father was happy about the union so he could keep tabs on James. It was his idea to end your life so Lola and James can marry legally. Between the two of them, they'll own 90% of the drug business in the United States. That's huge! Unfortunately, you were a casualty of war in the eyes of the DEA. I begged them several times to let me put you in protective custody, but they just couldn't risk it. It was a tough call, but in the end, the right one to take him down. Not only will we have him on attempted murder, but we'll also have him on several drug charges. We have another agent on the inside and he's been working for James as well. He is going to testify against James as will I."

There was a moment of silence while I was processing all of this. Right now I feel hurt, angry and thankful all at the same time. Despite all Bert has done for me, I'm mad at him for not helping me sooner. I'm scared for what can happen to him once James finds out and I am also thankful he is helping me. But mostly, I'm scared. I'm tired mentally, physically and just downright exhausted. I can't imagine a day without fear. Will my life ever be normal? So many emotions right now. I feel like my life is in a state of turmoil.

We rode in silence most of the day with an occasional food and restroom stop. I didn't have much of an appetite, but Bert did as usual. That man is always hungry. It's late and the sun has set. I pulled my hoodie over my head and sunk down in the seat. I turned the seat warmer on high and pulled my blanket over top of me. I'm just going to close my eyes and sleep. I don't want to think at all about anything for a little bit.

CHAPTER 6

Iwoke early. We were parked at a rest stop. I have no idea where I am and Bert is asleep. I just watched him sleep for a while, wondering what these years have been like for him. Obviously he has some human like feelings. He was genuine when he looked out for me, and he did eventually get me out of there. So I'm assuming it has been a rough time for him too. I'll try not to be so hard on him today. I wonder if he wants me to call him Bert or Mac? I guess I'll have to ask. I'll also be asking him again where he is taking me. He has not yet answered that very important question. I want to know and I'm not accepting the run around. And quite frankly I'm tired of sitting in his SUV. I need a hot shower and a bed to sleep in. I could feel a slight anger beginning to take over.

I looked over at Bert to see if he was awake and he was staring at me. He must have known what was coming next out of my mouth because he asked if I was ready for a hotel. I answered with a definite yes.

"How much longer are we driving before we get there, and where are we going, Bert?" My tone was curt. I'm tired of being the weak, fragile woman. I feel like I am gaining in strength every day. Must be the regular meals? I'm not sure but I'm actually feeling kind of amazing other than I feel dirty. I really need a shower.

We grabbed some breakfast and a cup of coffee and headed to the hotel. "I'm going to get you checked into your room and then I need to check in with James."

My legs instantly went weak. "Why?" I asked.

"I need him to believe it's happening tonight." He did a quick walkthrough of my room to make sure it was safe. He told me no calls from the hotel, no calls in or out and no exceptions. He then asked me to please stay in my room. I assured him I would comply.

Silence. Fear. Weakness. All at once! It's all I could feel. I'm such a mess! I was so glad to be alone for a little while. A good cry might be in order. I need to process what is happening. I need to take a shower. I need sleep. I popped a few Tylenol PMs and turned on the shower. I waited a few minutes for it to get really hot and I scrubbed my skin with soap, washed my hair twice. I felt so dirty after a few days without washing. But clean has never felt this good. I threw on a super big cozy sweatshirt and a clean pair of panties, my big fluffy socks and crawled into bed. I was asleep in seconds.

• • • • •

"Hey, James, it's Bert. Everything is going according to plan. We're almost there." The message was brief. The next call is to my real boss at the DEA. I'll be so glad when this case is over. It's been a long, hard road trying to put James behind bars. Watching the evil things this man has done to Jenna, his son and so many others has almost made me lose faith in the human race. I've had so many sleepless nights worrying if James was going to kill Jenna before we had something concrete to arrest him. He's been talking about it for a long time. I'm just glad she didn't become like him. She stayed true to who she really is, a smart beautiful woman who wants a simple life. I hope I can give that to her.

Tomorrow we'll arrive in South Carolina. We took the long way getting there so I could make sure we weren't being followed. I'm going to take Jenna to the beach at Pawleys Island. I hope there she'll find hope, peace and a seashell. She told me she's never seen one in real life. Neither a beach nor a seashell. It's about a 20-hour drive from Austin to Pawleys Island, but it took almost three days going the back roads. Once there, we'll meet my brother for the handoff. I haven't shared this part with Jenna yet. I'm taking baby steps with her, so that hopefully she trusts me enough now to know that she can trust him too. My brother's name is Mike, and he looks just like me, only about fifteen years younger. Handsome if I do say so myself. He's never been married except to his career. He's with the FBI, and she'll stay with him in a beach house that's been rented under an alias for the next year. Or until the trial of James is over and he's where he belongs. He'll be arrested tomorrow along with Lola. Right after I tell him the job is done. I'll fly back in the morning to deliver the news. I have a new truck registered to Bert. Hopefully James won't push for details. I'll make sure he understands why I can't give him specifics. He only needs to know her body will never be found.

In the meantime, I'm going to take a hot shower myself and get some sleep. We have a long day tomorrow. I set my alarm for 4 A.M. We need to be back on the road early. We're meeting Mike at noon at Pawleys Pier. I'll need to get gas, grab a bite to eat and check in with Mike. It would be nice if everything goes as planned, but honestly I'm expecting a few bumps along the way. If I plan for the bumps but if it ends up going smoothly then we can celebrate a successful transfer. Sometimes it's just a mind game you have to play with yourself to make it all work.

Hopefully Jenna gets a good day/night of sleep. I locked her door from the inside and put a ring camera at her door so I can look in on her throughout the night and make sure she's safe. We have adjoining rooms, but she knows I'm here if she needs me.

A few minutes have passed, and I just checked on her again. She's sound asleep. I don't think she's moved since the last time I checked over an hour ago. I left her a salad and a Coke in case she wakes up hungry for dinner. My guess is that she will sleep through the day and night. She seemed exhausted as am I. We both could use a good night of sleep, but I'll sleep much better once she's with my brother. I'm a bit worried that she'll be angry with me for not telling her, but I think it's for the best. I'll deal with her when the time comes.

I can't focus on the task at hand while I'm constantly worrying about Jenna. Once she's safe with Mike, I can strictly focus on getting James in custody. Sometimes I think this job will be the death of me.

Chapter 7

I woke up sad around 2 A.M. and started to cry. I cried for my son, and the thought of never seeing him again breaks my heart. There's this soul-crushing ache that is unmistakably grief for the son that was never really mine. Will time ease this pain? I hope so. He'll never know how much I truly loved him. Did I realize what I signed up for? Will never seeing him again be worth my life? I have to believe it is. I can never call him or hear his voice again. He'll be a memory. I sobbed some more and then pulled myself together. Who am I kidding? I knew exactly what I was signing up for. I need to remember how he has treated me. I need to remember who his father is and what he's capable of. Even if James goes to prison, his son, my son, would most likely retaliate. If he ever finds out I'm still alive, he'll be incredibly angry. I'll do my very best to make sure he never knows I'm alive. Maybe someday I can watch him from afar. Just a quick peek to make sure he's okay. For now, I'll just keep that thought to myself.

Right then I saw the salad sitting on the table with a note from Bert telling me to enjoy if I woke up hungry. All the sudden I was starving and realized I hadn't eaten since breakfast the day before. I devoured the salad, drank my Coke and then took another glorious hot shower. I fixed my hair, put on some make up and got dressed. I'm feeling much better, and looking better I think. I knocked on Bert's door. He answered right away as if he'd been up a while. He definitely smelled freshly showered. He wouldn't look me in the eyes right away so I know he's getting ready to be the bearer of more bad news, not a great way to start the day.

"Now what?" I said.

"What do you mean?" he replied.

"I've been around you enough over the last few days to recognize when you're getting ready to deliver bad news. And I thought you were the detective. Now spill! What do you have to tell me?"

He smiled and said, "I must be getting too old for this shit. I need a new line of work. Hell, I may just retire when this is done." Then he chuckled.

I've learned to really love his smile. He's been my savior, and I'm realizing just how much I needed him through all of this. I wonder if we'll stay in touch somehow when it's all over. If it's ever all over. My mind shifted back to the question. "I'm waiting," I said.

He replied by telling me that we have a couple more hours on the road. "Let's get packed up, get gas and grab a bite. Then once we're back on the road, I promise all the details. Agreed?"

"Do I have a choice?" I mumbled under my breath. Again he just smiled. I know I should be worried but I'm just not. What a weird feeling to not be scared or concerned. My instincts are telling me it's going to be alright. I feel pretty good right now. Is this what happiness feels like?

We stopped for gas first and then pancakes. Bert could not believe I've never had a pancake with maple syrup. He insisted I try them. And boy am I happy that I did. What delicious little flat cakes. I love them. Quite possibly the best thing I've ever had to eat. These tasty treats will be a regular on my menu! We'll just call these happy cakes from now on. How can a little cake make me feel this good? Even more amazing! We laughed about how excited I was over a pancake and then he paid our bill and we left.

On the way out, I was thinking about my childhood. I came from a family of losers. We never had food in the house, and my clothes reeked of cigarette smoke. I was the kid who had the free lunch tickets which I never used because I was too embarrassed about being the poor kid. My mom cared more about my stepdad of the month than she did me. Eventually I ended up in foster care, although there wasn't much difference between foster care and home. Boxed macaroni and cheese, SpaghettiOs and cold cereal were the staple. So when I met James, it seemed as though my life had taken a turn for the better. He made me feel special. I was sixteen when I married James. If only I knew then what my life was going to be like... I would have definitely made different decisions. But here we are. There are no do-overs in life, but there are second chances.

We were quiet for a few minutes once we were back on the road. I was going to let him share whatever he had to say when he was ready, but it didn't take long before he started to speak.

"Listen, Jenna, I'm taking you to meet someone else who is going to take care of you for a while."

Again… Fear.

"Why?" I asked. "Do you know this person you are taking me to?"

Bert replied, "His name is Mike. He's with the FBI, and he's my brother. He's just as committed to this case as I am. He's been working this case almost as long as I have been. He'll take good care of you… I promise. You're going to get a new name, a whole new identity. I need you to understand, this new identity is forever. You cannot contact anyone from your past, including family but especially your son. I saw you crying on the camera this morning, and I need to make sure you understand how important this is. Your son is involved with your husband's drug business. We are 100% certain of his involvement but are not going to arrest him. At least not right now. James, Lola and her father are the primary targets for now. Please tell me you understand." I shook my head yes as a tear ran down my cheek, indicating that I understood.

"Good," he said. "Under your seat is a large black duffle bag. Pull it out and open it up." I was shaking but did as instructed and was shocked at what I saw. I looked from the bag then back to Bert in disbelief. I was at a loss for words and said nothing. I simply stared waiting on him to speak. "This is every dollar paid to me from James for all the jobs I've ever done for him. There's almost 3 million dollars in there. I want you to have it to start your new life. It's also my way of apologizing for not being able to help you sooner. God as my witness, I tried. In the side pocket is a wallet with your new identification, along with your own phone. Your name as of today is Holly Tucker. You are thirty-five years old, no kids, no husband, no family, moving to Pawleys Island for a lifestyle change. You inherited some money after your grandmother passed. Remember the story. Rehearse it, know it and own it. Can you do that?"

It was so much to process. Holly Tucker. Do I even like this name? After pondering it for a few moments, I decided it has a nice ring to it. Financial security is a bonus. Wow! I'm really going to be free… sort of. Eventually, I guess, after James goes to trial. But he has people that will seek revenge. Or will they celebrate? Every day has something new to process. But first things first.

"I don't know how to thank you for everything you've done for me. For being there when I needed a friend and a protector. And now for giving me my freedom. How does one repay such generosity?"

"By staying safe," he said. "Just live a beautiful life. Make choices that will bring you longtime joy. You deserve it," he said.

I cried again but not because I was sad but because I can finally see a different life for me. But deep down I'm questioning, do I really deserve it? I mean, I made my decisions all by myself. Young or not, I should have known better.

Bert grabbed my hand and held it for a little while as we were driving. We were quiet but mostly because we both were feeling happy about the current situation. I couldn't help but smile. I felt like how a child is supposed to feel at Christmas. Yes, this is most definitely happiness. A feeling I've learned to recognize as of late and I really I like it.

Even though this is the shortest day of driving, it feels like the longest. I'm guessing because I'm so excited. I'm also a bit nervous. Even if Bert's brother resembles him in appearance, what will he be like as a person? Is he kind and caring like Bert? Will he make me feel safe? As I was all wrapped up in my own thoughts, Bert said we're almost here. Just as he said that, I smelled a smell I didn't recognize. A glorious smell. Bert pulled over and told me to close my eyes. He put a blindfold around my eyes and told me no peeking. We have about five more minutes until we get there. My heart skipped several beats. This is really happening.

I could hear Bert calling someone. "I'm almost there with the package," he said talking in code in case someone was listening in. I was being referenced as a package. Not sure how I feel about that. Maybe a bit annoyed. The call was brief and then he said, "I'll see you at the drop off point. We're getting close." My heart is pounding so hard and I began to shake. Bert said, "It's the adrenaline. You're okay."

About a minute later, we parked the car. The smell was amazing. I could hear birds, and then water. We got out of the SUV and started walking a short distance. Bert told me to stop and he took off my blindfold. I was speechless. Never ever have I seen anything this beautiful. It was all I had imagined it would be. And then some. Bert said, "Take off your shoes, let's take a walk." I happily obliged. My feet hit the sand. It was warm, soft and squishy… I let my feet sink in for a moment. This is beyond happiness, bliss perhaps? The water was the most beautiful blue color. The sun was warm and bright with a light breeze blowing the tousled waves of my hair. We started walking towards the pier ahead.

"We're going to meet my brother and then we'll have lunch and spend the afternoon on the beach. I have a flight to catch later, but Mike will take you to the next location. Are you good?" he asked.

"I'm way past good." I smiled so big my mouth hurts.

Bert introduced me to Mike. By all accounts, he seemed perfect just like Bert. He handed me a seashell and told me it was a perfect conch shell and that it was vacated by its previous tenant. He made sure to highlight that he would never take one with life inside. It made me giggle out loud and then I promised to never take one with a live tenant. It made me realize the importance of all life forms, even the tiny ones. I love the way he thinks. After lunch I'm going to spend some time searching for seashells. I'm so excited.

We had lunch at the Islander Bar and Grill. All three of us ordered the fried shrimp. It was absolutely fantastic. They were laughing and chatting about so many things from their jobs to childhood memories. I just sat back and watched them. How amazing it must feel to have a solid family. I was excited just watching them. They have a sister too. Her name is Kristy, and she was born in between them. A few years younger than Bert. She has two kids that are twelve and fourteen. I wonder if I'll ever meet them. I hope so. As I was watching them together, the waitress came by to ask if we wanted another drink. Of course I said yes. Who doesn't want another margarita? Especially when you're at the beach!

Mike asked me if I was ready for an afternoon at the beach.

"I'm definitely ready," I replied.

"Good, you're going to love it. I brought you a few beach necessities since you didn't know where you were going." He handed me a raffia bag and told me to have a look. "Let me know if you need anything else."

"Pinch me please," I said. "This whole day feels unreal to me. Thank you so much." I opened the bag and found a beach towel, some Hawaiian Tropic suntan oil, a bottled water and a sun hat. But the best thing in the bag was a little pouch for my seashells. I was so tickled. I could see they were both pleased with my reaction.

We headed back to the SUVs and drove back to the beach. I needed a swimsuit so they stopped at a little shop. I told them I would be right back. They weren't going to have it and told me they needed to go with me. Witness protection means no alone time. Well okay then. We all went into the shop. It was really funny having two grown men help me shop for a swimsuit. We were all in agreement, a black one piece with a low front and high thighs. I found the cutest black and white polka dot cover up dress that could be worn alone as a dress or as a cover up. I also found a pair of black bling flip flops. Just perfect to go with my perfect day! Luckily the hat is white with a black band, the beach towel is black and white striped and the bag is raffia with black handles so it all matches perfectly. I changed in the back seat since I can't be alone. They stood guard outside. The windows are tinted so no one could see in. I pulled my hair into a loose ponytail before putting my hat on. I took a quick glance of myself in the mirror, and I must say I look pretty darn cute. I laughed at myself.

When I stepped out of the SUV, they both were staring at me.

"What?"

"You look beautiful," Mike said, and Bert agreed with a nod.

"Thank you! I appreciate your kindness." I giggled because today I feel beautiful. I could definitely feel that Mike was attracted to me. And not in the same way as Bert. Bert was more like a dad, but Mike… it just feels different.

Chapter 8

The beach was absolutely perfect. It was warm and the waves were gentle. I am loving every moment of this new experience. Bert spent time on his phone working, and Mike walked with me collecting shells and educating me on what kind of shell they were. I did find a small conch without life. I was so excited I squealed with joy! Apparently quite loud because people were looking at me, but I didn't care. The excitement was real. I wrapped it in a tissue to keep it safe and placed it gently it in my seashell bag. I had quite the haul for my first time out. I can see this will be a favorite pastime for me. Quite possibly an addiction in the making. I was tickled by my own thoughts.

We sea-shelled for several hours, and then Bert came over to us to tell me he had to go stating he was heading back to Texas. "Mike, call me if anything changes and I'll do the same. In the meantime, Holly, you stay safe and stick to the plan. No deviations, no calls to anyone from your past, including me. I mean it. It's for your own protection." He hugged us both goodbye and walked back to his SUV. I felt a bit sad watching him go wondering if I'll ever see him again. I certainly hope so. He's been my rock, and I'll miss our daily talks. He's a good man.

Holly…so weird to have a new name. It will definitely take some getting used to. I guess I need to start calling Bert by his real name, Mac. He'll use his real name and I'll have an alias. Funny how things work out. He hasn't said any-thing about me still calling him Bert. But I guess to me he'll always be Bert. I'm starting to panic about him leaving. Oh no. I think I feel sick. Mike must have sensed my fear. He walked over to me and wrapped his arm around my shoulder. "I'll protect you, I promise. More sea-shelling or are you ready to go?"

" I guess that depends on when I get to come back," I said with a smile.

"You'll be able to come every day. That's our place, the blue building on the right. We're on the third floor."

"How exciting," I said with an enthusiastic tone. "I would love to see our place. Actually I think I'm ready for a nice hot cup of coffee and a shower. I have chills all of the sudden."

"Well, the sun is going down and you probably got a little too much sun for your first day out," he replied. "We'll get you a higher SPF sunblock tomorrow." I followed him to the beach exit wishing the day wouldn't end. It's wonderful to know I'll get to spend time here for the next year at least. It's incredibly beautiful. I can't even believe this is my life right now. Less than a week ago, I was banished to a room with an abusive husband.

We took the stairs to the third floor. He said, "We're never going to use the elevators. Even though we're in the off season for the beach and the tourist population is currently low, the less people who see you the better. Please do not leave the condo without me."

"I understand," I replied. Into another prison, I was thinking to myself. But I realize it's the only option right now and worth it for the long run. At least it's not an unhappy state like before. These views are spectacular, and Mike did say we'll get to come to the beach every day if I wanted to. And I'm sure I want to! Not even a question, I was thinking.

He opened the door to our condo, room 321. Stunning was the first thing that came to mind. It was decorated in beachy hues of coral, aqua and blue with lots of white and a sand/tan color. Perfection… oh, and did I mention the view? The excitement grew inside. I don't think I'll be able to sleep a wink.

Mike could see how excited I was and said, "I'm glad you approve," with a big smile. "Your room is at the end of the hall to the left; mine is on the right. I gave you the beach side room. I'm sure you'll be comfortable," he said, again with a big grin.

"I am certain I will as well," I said in agreement. "Thanks again, Mike."

•　•　•　•　•

She's really beautiful, so childlike and innocent when she experiences something new. I imagine this is truly incredible for her given all she has endured.

Her hair is just past her shoulders, medium blond, and she has the most amazing blue eyes. She's thin, maybe 5" 4' in height, and after today she's got a healthy, sun-kissed glow. Again, beautiful but she doesn't know it. As I'm watching her, I realized I want to kiss her. Clearly I should not be having these thoughts right now. What kind of protector am I? Disgusted with myself, I headed for the shower.

•　•　•　•　•

Well, that was weird. He just went to his room without saying a word. Maybe he's got private business he doesn't want me to know about. I need to take a shower anyway, and I'm ready to get comfy. A big sweatshirt, leggings and fluffy socks with a hot cup of coffee should do the trick. I'll unpack tomorrow.

I finished my shower and got dressed and went to the kitchen hoping Mike had some coffee. He was freshly showered also, and my goodness he smells amazing.

"Do you have coffee?" I asked.

"Yes, it's in the top cabinet over the coffee pot. If you need anything from the store, please let me know. We can go tomorrow if you like."

"That sounds great," I replied.

"I'm going out to drink coffee on the balcony, care to join me?"

"I would love to."

"Are you hungry?" he asked. "I can whip a little something up if you are."

"Actually, I'm not for some reason. I think I'm going to turn in early after I finish my coffee. It's been an exhausting few days." We sat quietly and just enjoyed hearing the waves crash below. Just slow enough to almost put you in a trance but not quite. This will forever be my favorite place. I don't know how I know this for certain, but I just do. I have never known such peace before, a calm I cannot explain. I went to bed in such a relaxed state, that I barely remember going to bed at all.

Chapter 9

I heard a knock on my door. Startled at first, I got up and opened my door. He stood there with a look of embarrassment and quickly turned away. In that moment I realized I was only wearing a long sweatshirt and white lace panties.

"I'm sorry for waking you," he said still not looking at me. "The tide is out and there are so many shells. Tomorrow there may not be any so I thought we could get down there early today before the other shell collectors arrive."

"Of course, oh my goodness! I'm sorry I answered the door half-dressed. I was not yet awake and the knock startled me. I'm so embarrassed."

"Don't be," he said. "This is new for the both of us. We'll figure out how to be roommates." He smiled big. "Get dressed and I'll get our coffee to go. How do you like yours?"

"Just black for me, please. A really big cup," I said, emphasizing really big.

He laughed again and said, "Got it on the really big part." He turned away and went to the kitchen.

He smelled so good again this morning. I opened my door and saw his big bluish-green eyes and that tousled dark hair. Tall, dark and handsome! Good grief, I'm in trouble. Is it wrong to be attracted to another man? As I'm having these thoughts, I can't help but wonder if I'm a horrible person. I mean, I am technically still married. But am I really married if I'm declared dead and have a new identity? Too early to think about this. I'm day five out of hell and already thinking about another man. I need to get ahold of myself. What is wrong with me! I should probably get checked out by a professional. My mind is all wrong. As I was scolding myself walking down the hall to the kitchen, he greeted me with our giant cups of coffee and asked if I was ready.

"I am," I said holding my emptied seashell bag. "What time is it anyway?"

"4:30 A.M."

"Oh," I said. "Do you wake up this early every day, or is this a rare thing? I'm just trying to prepare myself," as I laughed about getting up this early.

"No, I am pretty much an early riser."

"Good to know, I said. "I'll make sure to sleep in my pants going forward to avoid a repeat of this morning." We both laughed again and headed for the door.

Keeping with the protective rules, we used the stairs. Once outside, the light breeze was refreshing. It was dark, but there was the glow of the moon shining down on the water as gentle waves lapped on top of each other. The beauty of the ocean has touched my soul like nothing I have ever experienced. I felt instantly giddy and happy. Mike was right, seashells were everywhere. I cannot even contain the feelings of joy I am experiencing right now. Mike used the flashlight on his phone to help us see. Even though the sun will rise shortly, it felt like the middle of the night. We had the beach all to ourselves.

"I think I'm going to need a bigger seashell bag," I said. "I have no idea what I'm going to do with all of these shells. They are so beautiful, all of them, even the broken unique pieces I picked up. I love them all.

He agreed. "I'm sure you'll think of something useful to do with them."

The sun began to rise. I was so wrapped up in searching for shells, I hadn't realized how many people had arrived. We went from being alone to very busy pretty quickly. I started to watch people and their expressions as they were coming on to the beach. Some you could tell it was their first time here, others are locals that live here, and some were fisherman looking for the big catch of the day. Some were seashell enthusiasts, family vacationers, and others were there to surf. But all of them, regardless of their reason for being there, were gloriously happy. Just like me. Is it the beach that makes them happy? Are their lives happy without the beach? I pondered this as I was collecting seashells.

I turned to look for Mike and I could see him watching me. He was close enough to watch me and protect me if necessary, but far enough to give me some space to just be free. My god, this man is a beautiful human being just like Mac. Why couldn't I have met them when I was younger? They feel like my family. How is that possible? I've only met Mike a few days ago and there is definitely something there. He feels it too, I know it.

He walked over to me with an intense look of admiration. He took my hand and asked me to walk on the beach with him. I happily obliged.

"No sea-shelling," he said. "Let's get to know each other, okay?"

"I think that's a great idea," I said.

We started walking and he said, "Tell me about yourself."

"Well, there's not much to tell. I've only just begun to live my life as you already know. I came from an indignant family, I believe was the reference word they used when I was a child. My mother had a new move-in boyfriend every other month, a drug problem and no money. I couldn't wait to get out, so when James asked me to marry him at sixteem, I was thrilled to get away from that life. He came from a wealthy family and he seemed to really love me in the beginning. I thought I loved him too. We had our son, and he hired a nanny. As time went on, he was busy traveling. The nanny was raising our son, and I was banished to my room for most of the time. Then a few years in, we got a new nanny named Lola. That's when the real hell started, and it progressed from there. I wasn't aware of his drug business until Mac told me recently. I was blind to it all, a fool I guess in hindsight. So, that's about all there is to tell. My whole life in a matter of minutes. What about you? Why an FBI agent?"

"My dad was DEA, retired now. He worked long, hard hours. I was proud of my dad and the life he provided for us. He loves my mama like she's the only thing that matters. I wanted to be like him. I wanted to make a difference. Mac was also like a second dad in a way; he's almost fifteen years older than me. My sister is twe;ve years older than me. I was an accident," he stated matter of fact, "but I was the beloved baby of the family. I loved my life. I'm sorry yours was not pleasant, and hopefully your fresh start proves that second chances are worth taking."

"I'm happy for you. Everyone deserves that kind of family life. Unfortunately, there are many that don't make it out. I hope someday I can make a difference too and help the ones who do."

"Despite the life you have lived, you are so kind and caring. You still have trust in other people, although I don't know how. Your first thoughts after getting away are about helping others. I admire that about you," he said.

My heart just melted at his words. "I want to be a good person. Life is not worth living if you can't see the good, be the good, or be the difference. Don't get me wrong, I had my dark days. Days when I didn't know if I could go on. But I had a son that I hoped would someday need me or want me in his life. Maybe my second chance gives me an opportunity to have more children, children that get to grow up in a home just like yours. I want it all, a loving husband, kids, a house and a dog, and I will not accept anything less. Not this time. I intend to make the most of my second chance. I will no longer live in fear of someday."

:With your determination, I can see a bright future for you. It's almost 10 A.M. already, and I'm starving. Ready for some breakfast?" he asked.

"I am. Where can we get pancakes?"

"How about I make you some?"

"Perfect," I said. We headed back to the condo still holding hands. My mind is racing while I'm walking. What will happen between us? Will there be a love story with a happy ending, or will he break my heart?

Right then then my dreamy thoughts were interrupted. Mike got a call from Mac.

"Things aren't going as planned," he told Mike. "I'm not sure he's buying my story. I told him she was dead and buried and I assured him her body will never be found. Somehow, something is off. I feel it deep in my gut."

Mike started talking and told him, "It doesn't matter anyway. James will be charged for the hit on her life. We're going forward with the arrest." Right then there was an extremely loud noise, sounded like a bomb went off.

"Mac, are you alright? Mac, say something. Mac!"

Silence.

"Something's wrong. Very wrong. Let's get you back to the room." While we were walking, he tried calling Mac back three times. No answer. "I have to go to the office," he said. "I need to find out what's going on. I need to make sure my brother is ok."

Oh my god, I hope there wasn't an explosion. I need Mac to be okay. My heart can't take losing him, either of them. They are my whole world right now.

We got to the room, and Mike was still making calls while grabbing some clothes and his guns. After he hung up, bag in hand, he told me he was flying back to Texas to see if Mac is alive and to find out what happened. "They've also contacted the Texas FBI unit to get over to the mansion ASAP. In the meantime, I know I promised you daily beach visits, but I really need you to please stay in the room until I get back. Please tell me you will do that. There is plenty of food, water and whatever else you may need. Trust no one right now, and I mean no one other than myself and Mac. You can get fresh air from the balconies."

"I can do that. Will you please keep me informed about what is going on so that I'm not worrying about the two of you. Come back to me and bring your brother please."

As he was walking out the door, I hugged him. I looked up to him and he kissed me. A deep passionate kiss. He said, "I'll be back for you." That was it, and just like that he was gone and I'm alone and scared once more. Did James find out that Mac was helping me and that I'm still alive? Will he come and find me to finish the job? What if he found out that Bert was an undercover agent. So many things to be scared about right now. My peace was short-lived.

I know I should eat something, but my stomach is in knots. It's only been a few hours, but I wish Mike would check in. Something is better than nothing. Now it sounds like it's getting very windy and it's starting to rain. Really hard. I went to the balcony to check the weather, and the waves are no longer gentle waves of water. More like big angry waves with white caps. The palm trees appeared to be leaning sideways. Oh dear God, when it rains it pours, literally. What is this, a hurricane, a tropical storm? Seriously, why now? It could have waited until Mike came back. I took a quick shower and threw some clothes on in case I needed to escape. I don't want another embarrassing half-dressed situation. I turned the TV on to the local news to see what's going on. Then I crawled into the bed with my phone to hopefully sleep until this passes. I'm in for a long night. Ugh!

<h1 style="text-align:center">CHAPTER 10</h1>

I don't know how, but I survived the night. Thankfully I managed to sleep without waking up too many times. The news said it was a tropical storm and there wasn't too much damage. A few trees were down and some power outages. Luckily, I still have power, otherwise it would maybe cause me to lose any sanity I have left. I just checked my phone and still no word from Mac or Mike. I checked the time, and it's 4:30 A.M. I hope this isn't becoming my new sleep cycle. 4:30 A.M.? Ridiculous. But I'm wide awake now so I need to find something to do to help pass the time. I really want to go to the beach… but I promised. Maybe I'll fix me a coffee and head to the balcony and clean the shells I have. Maybe sort them by kind. I like it. It's been decided. It will keep me busy for hours.

I headed to the kitchen and fixed my coffee first. Grabbed the biggest bowl I could find and filled it with water and a squirt of dish soap. I carried both outside and went back in for my seashells. I didn't realize just how many I had. I'll definitely be busy for some time! Still excited about my shells, I started gently dumping them in the bowl. A little at a time to protect them from breaking. Or so I hoped. One by one I rinsed them and laid them all out on my beach towel to dry. Still no calls from Mike or Mac. I'm so worried. I don't know what to do. What if they're both dead? Did James pay someone off to disclose my location? Mike did leave a gun here, but will I even be able to use it? I've never fired a weapon in my life. Mike was going to teach me, but we didn't get to that in the short time we were here.

So now I'm back to waiting and worrying. What I will say is if they're both okay, and I hope they are, they're getting a serious scolding for causing me this much worry. We're approaching the 24-hour time of no word from anyone. In a worry world, that's an eternity. Moving to a pissed state of mind right now. They both might wish they never met me.

I realized I haven't eaten in over 24 hours. I went to the kitchen to make me a sandwich. Right then I heard someone at the front door. I thought it was Mike and almost opened it. Then I heard two men talking.

One said, "I've been watching the place, I haven't seen her leave. She's here."

Oh my god. I knew it. James sent someone to get me. Mike told me there is a secret door in the pantry. It's used to hide drugs temporarily when the DEA needed a stash house. I could still hear them picking the lock. I grabbed my bag, the one with my money and ID, the gun and went in the pantry. I opened the second door, which has a latch behind the jar of spaghetti sauce, crawled inside then pulled the door closed being careful not to knock anything down on the pantry shelf. The space is small, but I fit. Oh my god, they're in. I feel like they'll be able to hear my heart pounding. One can only endure so much! I mean good grief already!

I could hear them opening and closing doors, all the while talking about finding me or James is going to be pissed. I recognized one of their voices. His name is Louie, and he works for James. I'm so scared. I had the gun pointed at the opening of the door just in case they knew about the stash hole. They stayed for several hours and then I heard the door close. But I was too afraid to come out. What if they only pretended to leave in hopes I was there and would come out of hiding but were really still there? Not a chance in hell. I'll stay in this hole for as long as it takes. Hopefully I won't need a bathroom break since I haven't eaten for over a day.

I was right! I hear footsteps. I can't take any more excitement of this magnitude. Enough is enough. I'm about to shoot someone! I really don't want to, though. Please, please, please just go away, I keep praying to anyone who will listen. Right now I guess it's just me. The pantry door is opening, and I hear the second latch. My heart literally skipped several beats as the door flew open. I am found. My hands were shaking as I was trying to put my finger on the trigger and tears were pouring. I couldn't see beyond my own tears. I looked up about to shoot, and I heard his voice. Mike! He reached for me and pulled me to his chest. I'm crying so hard that I began to shake beyond my control. I nearly collapsed from the adrenaline rush. Mike held me steady and close as he whispered several times, "You're all right, you're alright. I'm here."

After a few minutes, Mike said, "We have to go. Quick. Grab your bags. There's a leak somewhere. We cannot stay here and we cannot trust anyone. I'm moving you, but no one is going to know." He asked me for my phone back, then pulled his phone from his pocket and smashed them both to pieces. I just watched him. He was frantically trying to get his things together, but I just stood there frozen in fear. "Jenna!" he yelled. "Get your things. Focus. We have to go!" Another tear rolled down my cheek and then I hurriedly grabbed my bags. Luckily I didn't get a chance to empty them to the dresser and closet just yet.

"I'll be quick," I said pulling myself together yet again.

We were both packed up in a matter of minutes and out the door. I headed for his truck, and he said, "Not that one. Follow me and stay close." We walked about a block I guess to a parking garage. We went to the second level and stopped at a covered vehicle. He pulled the cover off of an older blue Dodge Charger. He said, "Get in. I'll get our bags." I did as he said, feeling numb and scared. I was trying really hard to focus on what he was saying once we were both in the car, but I just couldn't. I didn't hear a word he was saying. I felt nonexistent. I swore to myself that I was going to be mad at him for not checking in, but I couldn't even make my mouth work. I just sat there with a mindless stare.

I don't know how much time had passed when I finally spoke. I simply said in a weak, exhausted voice, "Where's Mac?"

"I don't know, but I think he's alive."

"Why didn't you call me yesterday? Do you have any idea what I have been through? I've experienced the worst storm of my life, I worried about you and Mac all night and then James's men found the safe house. I was in that tiny space for hours terrified I was going to be found and killed. All that and you didn't feel the need to check in to let me know if you were safe, if Mac was alive or dead? What possible excuse could be nearly good enough?"

"Oh god, Jenna. I assumed you had a rough night, but I had no idea to what extent." He reached for my hand and I pulled away. "I couldn't call you," he said, "or I promise you I would have. I knew by the then our phones were tapped and I didn't want to put you in danger. Mac and I never talked about your location on the phone so I didn't think you were in danger. I'm still trying to piece together what happened and how they found us. I know for sure at this point, someone from the FBI is on James's payroll. Someone who's been following Mac to make sure he did his job. And when he found out that you were still alive with Bert's help, he sent a crew after Bert. I'm certain he is in hiding. I didn't find Mac's body, but he left me something at the bomb scene. We always said if we were in danger, we would leave our watch behind with location coordinates saved in the notes app. When I arrived at the scene, Mac's watch was lying under the mirror of his rental truck. The truck was burned, but his watch looked like it was placed there unscathed. He knew I would find it. There was no one there by the time my partner and I got there. James knew we were coming and he's long gone again. Something like this happens every time we're close to an arrest. I am 100% certain he's been getting a heads-up prior to our arrest plans."

He finished speaking and I apologized for my harsh tone towards him. "I do understand what you're saying. It sounds like the last 24 hours have been tough on the both of us. So now what? What are the coordinates on Mac's phone telling you."

"He's going to Mama's cabin on the lake in Cumberland, Kentucky. No one has been there for some time. If he's going there, something is wrong. Maybe he's hurt. I just don't know, but his phone is going right to voicemail. We're heading to the cabin too. We need to see if he's hurt. Otherwise he would be looking for James. That's not like him to just take a break at the cabin in the middle of a manhunt. I know from the last time Mac and I spoke, he was hell bent on making the arrest. Below the cabin is an old room, kind of like a cellar. From the cellar, there are tunnels that lead to a waterfall. It's believed by my mama that it was used as a way to hide and or escape from the Cherokee Indians should they come to the cabin. No one really knows for sure, but we let Mama believe what she wants."

We drove all the way through, a little over eight hours with one stop for gas and a bathroom break. It was a really long, long drive, or so it seemed. We didn't talk much. I think we are both consumed with worry for Mac. I just hope he's okay. And what about James? He won't stop until he finds me and finishes the job. I'm assuming James knows my new identity. Mike says there's a leak, and I'm inclined to believe him based on what has happened. So if that's the case, how can I possibly hide? I'll never be free. I almost started to cry again. I'm tired of riding the emotional roller coaster.

We turned down what appeared to be a very long dirt road. Mike turned off the headlights just in case someone other than Mac was at the cabin. I think the dirt road went on for about five miles. I could see a cabin in the near distance. It was dark, no lights.

"I don't see Mac's car," Mike said. "He also has a backup car like me, an older Chevelle in antique green. Given both of our career choices, it's always good to have a car that can't be tracked. Good old American cars, no technology for tracking, just the way I like it. Plus the car shows are fun," he said lightheartedly. "We'll have to go sometime."

"Sounds fun," I said.

We stopped a short distance from the cabin, and Mike told me to wait in the car.

"Really?" I said. "I don't think so. I'm coming with you. It can't be any less dangerous for me if someone does a little sneak sneak up on me and I'm alone. One experience like that was enough. I'm coming," and I opened my door. "What kind of protector are you?"

Mike just shook his head as if to surrender. He said, "Put this on. You can't do a 'sneak sneak' if you're glowing in your bright white shirt. This black one will be better."

"Thanks," I said and slipped it over my head. It smelled like him, and I instantly felt better. Almost felt like a hug. I smiled in contentment.

We started heading towards the cabin. Mike looked in the front window and didn't see anything. We walked around to the back. Nothing. Very quiet. Mike used his key and opened the door. All the sudden I felt a gun pushed in my back. I screamed and then I heard Mac say, "What the hell is she doing here? Did you really think this was the best place to bring her?"

"Where did you think I should take her?" Mike said. "They damn near found her today. Thank god for the stash house room or she'd be dead right now."

"Are you guys really having this conversation as if I'm not here? I'm just about done with the both of you. I'm probably safer without you," I said with tears welling up in my eyes.

"I'm so sorry," they both blurted at the same time.

Then Mike started speaking to Mac. "The safe house was found today. Jenna hid in the stash closet. Luckily they didn't find her. Apparently, they went for you and then her. I'm going to assume my cover is blown as well. There is no way James doesn't have somebody on the inside with the DEA and the FBI. The question is who. I know I haven't shared any information about this case with anyone. I'm going to assume you haven't either, Mac. So who knows about the safe house besides us?"

Mac said, "I know Alex is your partner and friend. What information does he have about this case?"

"As far as I know, no one else was working this case or had any information about Jenna," Mike said. "So it's either the captain or it's my partner. Somehow I can't see it being the captain. Alex has been a little different lately. Going off on his own, taking calls in private. I can't believe I didn't pick up on it."

Just then, Mac put his hand to his rib and winced in pain.

"Damn, Mac, you've been shot," Mike said.

"Don't I know it," Mac replied with a halfhearted laugh. "This shit hurts."

"Oh my god," I said. "What can I do?"

"Actually Mama is here. She's in the cellar setting up to take the bullet out. I came up here when I heard the door."

I must have had a terrified look. One because I am terrified and two he should be going to a hospital.

Mike said, "Mama is a nurse. She's done this before. We've both been shot a time or two. It comes with the job." He stated this matter of fact. As if it's normal to get shot and call your mama. Who are these guys? Do I really even know them at all?

"Let's get you down to Mama."

Mike and I both helped him down the steps to the cellar just before he passed out.

"Hey, Mama," Mike said. "Good to see you."

"Likewise, my son. Your brother has lost a lot of blood. I'm going to need your help."

I was frantic, physically sick to my stomach. I don't think I can be in here. Mike's mama told me to go back upstairs and keep watch. Just in case they find our location. "Take the shotgun," she said.

"Mama, I don't think she can handle a shotgun."

"Well, unless she wants to help remove the bullet, we need her to keep watch upstairs." He didn't disobey and nodded to me to go upstairs as instructed. I gladly did so. My heart was racing from fear, worry and anxiety. But his mama seemed stern and confident. Nothing like me. I'm weak, fragile and timid. I guess the life you live determines your characteristics. His mama is petite in height and weight, long gray hair pulled back in a messy bun. She has those same beautiful eyes as Mike and Mac. Probably a real catch back in the day. She's certainly still attractive for a mature woman. I'm guessing she's always been able to hold her own, no matter what the situation may have been. How lucky they are to have been blessed with such a woman for a mama.

I don't know how much time has passed, but the sun is beginning to rise. Their mama came upstairs to tell me, "Mac is gonna make it. Mike is watching over him. He'll need a few days to rest." I almost burst with excitement. "I'm Maggie by the way, but everyone calls me Mama. You can too if you like. Sounds like you've had a tough time the last few days. Mike filled me in with all of the details."

"I'm sorry," I said. "I didn't mean for my situation to cause any problems for your family."

"No worries, dear. I've accepted their line of work. It took a few bullets and sleepless nights to understand why they chose their line of work. I'm proud of both my boys. I'm not just being the proud mama, they've worked hard and have made a difference in the world. Put lots of bad people where they belong. No mama can ask for more than that. I'm gonna shower," she said. "Why don't you see what you can find to eat in the kitchen."

I almost panicked. I have no idea how to cook. Holy shit. But like Mac and Mike, I did what she said. I already admire her. How did she do that?

I went to the kitchen and started opening cabinets. They were stocked with food for days. I saw two cans of Spam, canned potatoes and powdered eggs. Biscuits were in the freezer, along with some butter. "Okay, I can do this," I said. I found several pans and turned the stove burners on. So far so good. I put the biscuits in the oven first. Next I diced the Span and added the diced canned potatoes. Added a little salt, pepper and butter. While that was cooking, I followed the instructions for the powdered eggs. Just then Mama walked in freshly showered.

"Smells fantastic," she said. "I'll let the boys know it's just about ready."

"Can Mac climb the stairs?"

"Don't you worry, we'll get him up here for this fine meal," she said with a smile. "Besides, the sooner he's up and moving, the better."

Chapter 11

I was feeling proud of the first real meal I cooked. Everyone seemed to enjoy it, including Mama. We all sat together like a family. There was talking and laughing. Funny how Mac seemed almost normal. He showed very little evidence of being in pain.

"Mama," Mac said, "I want to go home for a few days. I'll rest best there I think. You cooking for me Mike and Pops. It'll be good, and besides, you know Mike and I will have to get back to work soon."

"Listen," she said, "there is nothing I would like more. But it's not safe to leave here just yet. I called Pops this morning. He's on his way here. Your sister and her family are coming too. We don't know if they'll come looking for you and her at the house. At least the cabin is not in our name. This cabin and all the land have been in our family forever, but my daddy said the land will remain in his daddy's name forever. It will be difficult for them to find us here. We'll take turns keeping watch just in case." And just like that, Mac and Mike agreed. The level of respect they have for their mama is amazing. My son never treated me with respect. For a minute I almost cried but quickly snapped out of it.

"Let's get Mac to his room to rest," Mama said. "I'll clean up the dishes and then run into town for a few things. Jenna, would you like to come with me?"

"Yes, ma'am, I would love to."

"But please don't call me ma'am. Mama or Maggie. You choose, but please not ma'am. Makes me feel older than I am." Then she laughed. "Mike, you stay here with your brother after you move your car down to the tunnel."

I took a quick shower and got dressed. I was a little nervous about being alone with Mama, but I couldn't put it off. Best to just move forward. Clearly, she wants to be with her kids, and if Mike and I are going to be together, I'll need her approval, as it should be.

We chatted along the way. She asked me about my family and my marriage. I wasn't sure what Mike and/or Mac had told her, so I thought it best to just be honest. No matter how uncomfortable it might be. "I'm embarrassed about my life," I told her. "Although, I'm not sure why. I didn't ask for this life. It was mostly handed to me. The one choice I did make sealed my fate. James, the biggest regret in my life. I can't help but wonder, if I was given a do over, how might my life have turned out. I try not to think like that too often because I can't get a do over and I can't change my past."

"No, you can't," Mama replied." But everything you do from here on out is up to you. You have been given a second chance. So many don't. Get married again, have kids that you can love, but most importantly love yourself and the rest should happen naturally. Just know, there is lots of evil in this world, but there is also lots of good. Be the good, and the good will follow."

"Thank you for today," I told her. "I can see why your children adore you. I think I like having a girls shopping day," I said with a smile.

We went to several boutique type stores. I found a dress I really liked but put it down. I decided I really didn't have anywhere to wear it.

Mama said, "You buy that dress, find you a cute pair of shoes to go with it and a matching bag. Every girl needs a dress that makes them feel beautiful. And this dress will not only make you feel beautiful, it will help you see how beautiful you really are. Besides, you're gonna need a few of them for church on Sundays when this chapter of your life is over."

I teared up. I never had a mama of my own to share such words of wisdom. "In case I forget to tell you," I said, "today was perfect." She smiled softly.

After we both purchased a couple of dresses and accessories, we stopped at the grocery store and bought lots of groceries. Enough for an army, I would say. I'm guessing we'll be at the cabin for quite some time. I offered to pay for them, but she wouldn't hear of it. On the way out, we grabbed a coffee and a pastry. She laughed and said, "This is why I like to grocery shop. I love me some pastries!" We both laughed in agreement.

We drove back to the cabin chatting most of the way, while eating our pastry and sipping our coffee. It was so nice having girl time. I've forgotten how fun that can be. We turned down the long dirt road heading towards the cabin. It looks so different during the day versus when we came in at night. It's absolutely beautiful. There are rolling hills of trees, tall grasses and a fairly wide stream. I didn't even realize we drove over a bridge last night. While the smell is not of the beach, it has its own unique smell. Like fresh, clean and airy. There is also a light breeze which feels amazing with our windows down. Content is the word that comes to mind.

We arrived at the house, and a woman came running out to greet us. "Mama, I'm so glad you're here. I've missed you," she said.

Mama laughed and said, "I miss you too, but you realize I just saw you day before yesterday."

Then I laughed. "How joyful watching all of you. I'm guessing you are Kristy, the sister and middle child."

She laughed and said, "Yes, I'm Kristy."

"A pleasure to meet you," I told her.

She replied, "It seems as though you've had a crazy time as of late. Let me tell you, you're in for an adventure when all of us manage to get together. You just may get more than you bargained for! Crazy lives here!" I instantly took a liking to her. Now that I've met all three siblings, I can tell they love each other deeply and I'm in for a great time. It doesn't seem to matter to any of them that their lives might be in danger. This is simply an opportunity to all be together. How perfectly beautiful, I thought to myself. I felt a rush of excitement similar to what I felt when I went to the beach. Another sampling of happiness.

An older gentleman greeted us at the door. He took the bags from Mama and kissed her on the cheek. So sweet. I looked around the room and saw Mike watching me. He blew me a kiss. The room was total chaos. People talking, grocery bags being tossed around, luggage and bags everywhere, but it appeared to be mayhem and happiness all mixed up. Mac was sitting in the chair looking exhausted. Was on my way over to him when some other lady beat me to it. Who is this, I thought. No one mentioned her in their stories. I stopped to turn around. and Mac summoned me to come on over. I bent down to hug him and asked if he's okay.

He replied, "I'm okay. A little sore and tired."

Just then the woman appeared and introduced herself. "Hi, I'm Sonja, Mac's girl."

"Oh," I said giving Mac a look for never mentioning her. He smiled back at me and had a look as if we'd be discussing this later. Not that he owes me an explanation or anything, but I am curious why he didn't mention her. It's weird, I found myself feeling protective over him. Maybe because he was he only person I really cared about for a long time.

Just then the older gentleman walked over. "Hello there, I'm Andrew, Mac's pop." He gave me a brief hug.

"Hello, I've heard so much about you. How are you?" I replied.

"I'm much better now that my kids and all their families are here. When Mama decided to go running off on her own, I was a little worried. But like always, she pulled our clan together and we're all safe. These are the moments Mama and I live for."

"I can see why; you have an amazing family," I said. "Lots to be proud of and more to be thankful for."

"Yes I do," he agreed. "Pleasure to meet you," he said. "I'm gonna go see if Mama needs me. Enjoy your time here and let us know if you need anything."

"I will," I said. I looked back to Mac. "You look tired. Can I get you anything?"

"A cup of coffee would be great."

I went to get Mac's coffee, and Mike greeted me halfway with a kiss on the cheek. I could feel his family watching us. I hope it's being received as positive. My mind always goes to being worried. I really need to work on that. I told him I was getting coffee for Mac.

He said, How about after you get his coffee we take a walk. It's beautiful outside and I want to show you something."

"Sounds lovely, but give a few minutes. I'll meet you out front." I took Mac his coffee and then went to my room and freshened up. I put on my new dress and looked in the mirror. I looked well put together, not at all how I normally look and dress. I think I could get used to wearing dresses. It's casual but feminine. I chose the one with a low front and spaghetti straps. It has small pink, green and blue flowers on an ivory background. Then I grabbed my denim jacket on the way out.

I could feel everyone looking at me. I turned to meet their gaze. Mama just winked at me. Everyone else was silent. Maybe I don't look as cute as I thought I did. I almost regretted choosing the dress, but then Mike met me at the door. The way he looked at me said it all. He definitely approved. He told me I was the most beautiful woman he's ever seen. I smiled and thanked him. Then he handed me a pair of boots. "You're going to need these for where we're going," he said. " It's rained a lot lately, and where I'm taking you tends to get muddy after a big rain. The boots are my sister's, but she won't mind if you use them. They may be a little big, but they should work."

I slipped a pair of socks on and then the boots. Mike was right. They were a little big but workable. Not sure they were a great match for my dress, but I just went with it.

He hollered in the front door to tell his mama we were taking a walk. She hollered back to us to be careful and enjoy the beautiful day. Out the door we went and headed left down a grassy hill.

"I love this time of year," I said. "It appears to be beautiful no matter where we go."

He looked at me and said again, "You're beautiful," and he took my hand. "I couldn't wait to have you to myself," he said with a smile.

"Well, you now have me all alone. What are your intentions?" I said in a soft, flirty voice. Weird how that just came out of my mouth, I was thinking. Who am I right now? Just down the hill there was a giant weeping willow tree. The most amazing tree I have ever seen. Miked pulled the hanging branches apart and we walked under it. I felt like a child again as the awe I was experiencing was again a new feeling to me.

"I love the sparkle in your eyes when you're excited," he said as he pulled me close and kissed me. I found myself kissing him back. I had this urgent need to be consumed by him. He felt the same hunger I was feeling. I started to take his shirt off, and he stopped me and said, "Not here. I want this to be special for us."

I looked at him and said, "This moment is special. This has been the most beautiful day of my life. I want you right here, right now under this tree." We started kissing again, and the clothes started coming off. I was scared and excited at the same time. We fell to the ground, and within moments he was inside me. I loved his smell and the sweet gentle way he made love to me. It seemed like we laid there for hours just holding each other, looking up inside the tree, talking about the history of the tree, the land and his family. He's very proud of his parents, for their life and the life they provided their children. He grew up in a very happy healthy family. Something I have longed for my entire life. I'm so happy for him.

"Shouldn't we be making our way to where you were taking me?" I asked. "Although this feels pretty perfect, your family might be asking what I thought of where you were taking me. I really don't want to tell them we never made it past the willow tree," I said with a grin.

"This feels like heaven," he said, "but you're right." He got up first and then helped me up. We stood there naked and kissed once more. I pulled away and grabbed my under clothes. "We both know where that was headed if I didn't stop kissing you." He simply smiled and grabbed his pants.

Once we were dressed, we started heading further down the hill. "I'm going to have to get in better shape if I'm going to climb hills, valleys and cross streams," I said practically out of breath.

"We're almost there. You're going to love it of this, I am certain. Ok, close your eyes."

"This must be a family thing. Your brother did this to me at the beach." We laughed and I closed my eyes.

A short distance later, he told me to stop and turn around and open your eyes. I did as he asked. I was looking at a cottage built halfway underground. It had a round front door with a tiny window. There were several other tiny windows on the front. He turned me the other way and we were on a river.

"Oh my goodness, this is beautiful," I told him. "Really it's amazing. Your family definitely knows how to live."

"While everything around us is family land, this little cottage is all mine. I was the baby and my grandmother adored me. She left it to me in her will. This was her getaway place when she wanted to be alone. It didn't feel right coming here 'til now. I know we don't know each other that well yet, but something about being with you feels perfect. It feels right and how it is supposed to be. You don't have to say anything right now. You don't don't have to feel the way I do and that's okay."

I walked over to him and kissed him with a deep passionate kiss. "I knew there was something between us the very moment I met you. I want to be a part of your life. I would love to see inside your grandmother's cottage."

He used his key to open the door. I was in awe once again. This tiny remote cottage was beautifully preserved with his grandmother's things. I felt like I took a step back in time.

The kitchen was nothing more than a nook. It had a small wood square table and four matching chairs. A sink, a very old vintage stove and refrigerator. No dishwasher. There were three wood shelves above the sink made from the same wood used for the table and chairs, along with a few wood cabinets, including a small pantry cabinet. They appeared to be a walnut-colored wood. There was a small braided rug in front of the sink with green and white hues. The sitting area boasted a small green plaid couch and a contrast floral footstool, as well as end tables keeping with the walnut finish. There was a bed in the back right corner with two small green dressers as nightstands. Lastly, there was an old claw bathtub, a white sink and commode in a tiny bathroom. It all matched beautifully. I wouldn't change a thing if it were mine. I can see why his grandmother loved it here. It's truly a beautiful place of serenity and peace.

"Mike, thank you for sharing this with me. It means so much."

"Spend the night with me here in the cottage," he said. "Let me make love to you all night long. I feel like I can't get enough of you."

I blushed a bit and said, "What about your mama? I don't want to disrespect her. What will she say about us spending the night together so soon?"

"My mama is the most down-to-earth person you will ever meet. She likes you and she'll be happy I've met someone who actually means something to me. I'm known as a bit of a player, but that's only because I've been looking for you all along," he said with that big beautiful irresistible smile. Then he winked.

"You sure know the way to a girl's heart. I would love to stay with you tonight in your grandmother's cabin. Am I going to wake up and the fairy tale is going to be over?"

"Absolutely not! This fairy tale is just the beginning, and I promise you a happy ending." We kissed again and I was feeling that urge to have him once again. "I'll be back," he said leaving me in this state of need. "I'm going to run back to the cabin and grab us an overnight bag. But hold on to that need. Make yourself comfortable, and I'll be back in less than an hour." Remembering that I'll have him all night will have to suffice until he gets back.

I went to the tiny bathroom. It was spotless as if someone had just cleaned it. I turned the water on and made it really hot. I then looked in the wood cabinet beside the bathtub for some soap and shampoo. I found everything I needed for a relaxing bath, to include a eucalyptus candle, lavender bubble bath, a razor, shampoo and lavender body oil. Towels and washcloths in a pale green were on the shelf over the toilet. I'm feeling very thankful for a hot bubble bath. There was a bottle of wine in the pantry so I poured myself a glass and then headed back to the bathroom and stepped into the tub. It was deeper than I thought, but that just made it better. I was in heaven.

I soaked for a little while before getting out. This feeling of clean is indescribable. Once I got out, I dried my hair but not all the way and pulled it up in a bun. Then I applied the luscious lavender oil to my skin. I took the candle to the bedroom area after I picked up the bathroom and rinsed the tub. Then I crawled into bed without any clothes. "Naked is feeling pretty good," I said to myself. I was waiting on Mike and must have dozed off. I didn't even hear him come in and get into the bed with me. I was awakened by him caressing and kissing my breasts. Now I'm definitely awake and feeling the need to feel him inside me once more. He climbed on top of me and began to move. This time not as gentle as the last. We made love for hours. I have never been loved like this. Loved to pure, sweet exhaustion. We slept through the night only to wake up and want each other again.

Afterwards, I told him I really needed a cup of coffee. He happily obliged and went to the tiny kitchen to make us some in an old percolating coffee pot.

"My goodness, that smells amazing," I told him in a louder than normal tone. I wanted to make sure he heard me from the back of the cottage.

"It sure does," he said walking back and handing me a cup. "After coffee, we'll head back to the cabin. I want you to get to know all of my family. They're pretty great, huh?"

"They certainly are," I agreed wholeheartedly.

"Before we go, I need to run something by you. I'm thinking when Mac and I head back to work in Texas, I want you to stay here with Mama and Pops. You'll be safe here. Just until we get James."

"You won't find him," I said. "He'll find us when you least expect it."

"Let's hope that's not the case," he said.

We took a quick shower, got dressed and then he grabbed our bag. We headed back to the cabin. "I feel like we're two teenage kids sneaking back in after staying out late," I said.

He laughed and said, "It kind of does, doesn't it?"

We opened the door and everyone looked up from what they were doing. Mike just grinned, and I'm pretty sure I was fifty shades of red.

Mama said, "I was just getting ready to come and get the both of you. It's almost breakfast time."

"What can I do to help?" I asked trying to divert the attention we were getting as well as the looks and grins. I'm sure they're all speculating about Mike and me.

Mama said, "Grab some plates and silverware for everyone." They had added the two leaves to the table. It was massive and made a serious statement in the dining room. It seats sixteen. This meant there was plenty of room to set the table for everyone with room to spare. This was a feast for the seriously hungry. I was feeling guilty about not being there to help prepare a meal such as this, but I'm definitely hungry. There were biscuits and gravy, sausage, bacon, eggs, fried potatoes, pancakes, orange juice and pastries of course. The smell of everything is making me so hungry. I was excited to see pancakes on today's menu. I'll have some of those first, I was thinking to myself.

We sat down to eat, all ten of us. Mama, Pops, me and Mike, Mac and Sonja, Kristy and Mark and their two daughters Ava and Ana. It got quiet for a moment while Pops said a quick prayer. He thanked God for their precious family and for the new family members at the table, for the food we were about to receive as well as keeping their family safe. As soon as the prayer ended, all manners went out the door. There were about five conversations going on at the same time, utensils clanging, serving bowls being passed and food flying. I just sat back and watched for a minute or two. It was loud, it was beautiful. I looked to Mama, and she just smiled at me. I started to eat and then I looked at Mike. He was genuinely happy. I am happy. My heart is beyond happy.

I'm not sure how many bedrooms are in the cabin, but I'm going to say at least five bedrooms and probably that many bathrooms. There's a large cobblestone fireplace in the center of the cabin. Everyone went to sit by the fire after breakfast where the chaos and conversation continued. There are no TVs.

I thought that was a bit odd, but Mama says the cabin is for family time. No phones allowed either. As I'm looking around the room, they all seem to be content just catching up.

I got up to go get another cup of coffee. Mac followed me into the kitchen.

"Hey," he said.

"Good morning," I replied. "How are you feeling?"

"Getting better. So you and my brother are a thing."

"I think we are," I said smiling. "He makes me happy. All of this makes me happy. Are you okay with me and Mike being together?"

"I am. Happy looks great on you. And besides, if you and Mike are together then I know you're okay. I wanted you to be safe for so long."

I thanked him again for everything he has done for me. We hugged briefly and then I asked, "So you have a girl?"

He grinned. "I do, but it's been an on-again, off-again kind of thing. She struggles with my line of work. Says I'm married to the job, which I kind of am, until all of this. I think once we get James, I'm done. I'm tired. And seeing you and Mike happy makes me really feel the need to settle down. Mama told Sonja that I was shot and that she needed to be in protective custody too. I was glad when she showed up. Since my cover was blown, Mama wasn't sure she was safe. Now I just don't know how far James's reach actually is."

"He's an evil man," I said. "I'm not sure any of us are safe."

He agreed but then said, "All that matters to me is here in this house. I can rest easy for a few more days, then the search will continue."

Chapter 12

The last few days have been bliss. Spending time with Mike, Mac and their entire family feels like I'm in dream. I've wanted this my entire life. The women have all been cooking and planning meals together including Ava and Ana, Mikes nieces. Mama baked a beautiful butter Bundt cake with lemon icing today. It looked and smelled amazing. Apparently, this is a family favorite, Mama's own recipe. I can't wait to have a piece. I'm drooling for sure. These small things are what make up family traditions. Will this be me and Mike's life someday?

Mike and I sneak away to the cottage when we can. But we are sharing a room at the cabin, as are Mac and Sonja. We want to spend time with the family too since all of them being together doesn't happen as often as they would like. It's certainly been a lot of fun despite everyone's reason for being there. While a bad situation has brought them all together, you would never know.

They play a lot of games, and it's funny how competitive they all are with each other. Mama saw me watching them and came over to me. She put her hands on my shoulders from behind me and whispered in my ear, "You belong here," and kissed me on the cheek. "Because of you, we get to have the entire family together. Thank you for that. Andrew and I are growing old. We wake up thankful every day that we're alive to see another day. And these right here are the days that matter." She smiled and walked away without giving me a chance to speak. I could almost swear I saw a tear run down her cheek.

In that moment, I did believe this is my family, my home and my life. But what happens when Mike and Mac have to leave and go back to work? I'm not so foolish to know it's inevitable. Mac is getting around pretty good now, and he has a strong desire to see this case through to the end. I used to be scared every day of my life and I still am I guess about some things. Only right now I'm scared for different reasons. I don't want anything to happen to Mike or Mac. And I don't want to lose this life. Mama and Pops are getting up in years. What will happen to their family when they're gone? I just can't bear the thought of this. I'm going to pray for them to have many more years.

Just then Mac and Mike appeared. "This can't be good," I said, "judging by the look on your faces."

"Mike just talked to his captain," Mac said. "They need him back, and I'm going to assist the DEA with this one. I'm going with him. James and Lola have to be stopped. We need our family to be safe once and for all. And we need to stop the drugs from coming into our communities. The captain said Alex has been arrested. There was plenty of evidence against him, but he was offered a plea deal. If he talked, he would get life in solitary confinement, and he took the deal because he knows he'd be a dead man in general population."

I looked at Mike because he hasn't said a word but is visibly upset. "Mike, are you okay with this?" I asked.

"I have to be," he replied. "I'm not going to lie. The thought of leaving you has my stomach in knots. I will never forgive myself if something happens to you because I left you here."

"Then let me go with you," I said.

"No, you can't," they both said in unison.

Mike continued. "This option is the lesser of two evils. Staying with my family is what's best."

"When do you leave?" I asked.

"Tomorrow morning," he replied.

Mac walked away and said he was going to tell Sonja and the rest of the family the grim news. Mike stayed with me. He apologized for having to leave me. I hugged him tight, and tears started to run down my cheek.

"Hey, please don't cry," he said. "I'll be back soon and we'll pick up where we left off. I know our relationship has been somewhat brief, but I'm in love with you already. You are all I think about. We need to get James and Lola or we'll never be free to have a life together. I have to do this for us."

I sobbed some more and then I told him I loved him too. "Please get that bastard," I said. "I'm ready to close that chapter of my life forever. You and Mac take care of each other and come home safe. Will you be able to check in with us from time to time?" I asked.

"No, I can't compromise your location, or that of our family."

"I understand," I told him. We went back to be with the rest of the family. This was the quietest it has been since we all got there.

Mama was in the kitchen cooking because this is what makes her feel good. I offered to help but she said no. This must be how she deals with her grief. As a mama, I would be worried too. For another moment I thought about my son and wondered how he's doing. By now, he knows I ran away from him and his father. There will be no words to ever help him understand why. I'm sure he hates me. Maybe I deserve it, maybe I don't. But his father will never let me be in his life. Even if he goes to prison, he'll have a firm hand on Junior without a doubt. There's just no easy way to make things right. Once again, I feel the ache of my broken heart. One I will likely carry until my last breath. I'll have to learn to manage my feelings between grief and happiness.

I went to our room to draw a hot bath, wishing I had the lavender from the cottage to take my worries away. There's just something about lavender that calms my inner self. Mike soon joined me in the bath. We were quiet while gently washing each other. Afterwards, we joined the rest of the family for dinner.

Mama made an amazing dinner. Fried chicken, mashed potatoes and gravy, green beans and homemade biscuits with apple butter. We all sat at the table and ate, but this time was different. Not much chatter, food being calmly passed, and everyone had a different look about them. One I recognize. The look of sadness and concern. The sparkle that was there not long ago is gone. It's hard to believe how two brothers leaving changed the entire family from lively and happy to complete sadness. This in itself is crushing. All I know is that Mac and Mike need to come home safe or this family will never be the same.

After dinner, everyone was in a solemn state of mind. No one stayed up for long. Everyone turned in for the night except Mama and Pops. They stayed by the fire and just held each other. Now that is a solid relationship and one I hope to have with Mike. They're strong because they deeply love each other and are there to hold each other up during times like these. No wonder Mike and Mac are so caring. They had the best teachers imaginable.

Mike and I laid in bed and talked until the wee hours of the night, until neither of us could keep our eyes open. I didn't want to lose any precious time that I had with him. Literally every second was a gift. No matter what happens, the time spent with Mike, Mac and his family over the last few weeks have been hands down the best days of my life. Just before I drifted off to sleep, I had one last look at the amazing man who lays beside me. Without a doubt, I'm in love with him. With all my heart and soul.

CHAPTER 13

Everyone was up and at it early. They were hugging each other goodbye and the tears were flowing, including my own. I couldn't help but feel like this was somehow my fault. If Mac wasn't undercover trying to catch my husband James, then this lovely family would not be saying their goodbyes at all. And Mama wouldn't be worried about two sons going off to fight a war of sorts. A war that can never be won. Sadly, drugs are everywhere, and with powerful people like James controlling the vast majority of imported drugs, there's no end in sight. Even if they lock James up in prison forever, someone will be there to take his place. So the war will go on. My logical side knows this, but my heart roots for Mike and Mac to take them all down one at a time. But my love for them wants them both to be done with the war and stay home where evil doesn't exist. I just don't know if either of them will really ever walk away from the only life they've ever known. A life that protects and serves. For now, I'll pray for their safety.

I stayed in our room because I don't think I can face his family. What if they begin to blame me too? I'm just so scared to lose what I now consider to be my family. I adore them all. Just then Mike came in to tell me goodbye. He held me tight and kissed my forehead. "Please stay in the house as much as possible. I don't know how long we'll be gone, but I'll come back to you as soon as I can. I love you," he whispered giving me one more kiss goodbye. I told him I loved him too and then he left.

All of this just seems so unreal to me. We were supposed to be safe staying in a beach house. Why couldn't that have worked out? But… then I most likely would not have gotten to know his family. I'm trying to believe things happen for a reason and will turn out how they're supposed to.

After some time alone, I decided to join the rest of the family. I have to face them sometime, so I'll just get it over with. Everyone seemed to be in their own thoughts today. Not at all how they normally are. This will be hard for me. I think I'll go to the cottage and on the way, spend a few minutes at the willow tree. Maybe some alone time is what I need. I told Mama I was going to the cottage and that I thought I would spend the night there. She nodded as if she understood. I went and grabbed a few items from my room.

When I was coming out, Mama handed be a brown paper bag. She said, "You may get hungry later so I packed a few things for you to eat later." My eyes teared up as I thanked her. My own mama never packed me a lunch, I thought. Mama told me to take as much alone time as I needed and that they were all there for me.

"Thank you… for everything," I replied.

I left the cabin with my things and headed to the cottage. But first stop is to the willow tree. I pulled aside the hanging vines just like before and went in. It really is the most unique tree I have ever seen. It's like being in a hut of sorts. For a brief moment I closed my eyes and thought about the first time Mike and I made love right here under this magnificent tree. I felt something I have never felt before: love for someone that is true and deep. I started to tear up, but this time it's tears of joy. I laid there and sobbed until I fell asleep. I woke up in a panic because it was almost dark. I grabbed my bag and came out from under the tree and headed towards to cottage. A little faster, I thought to myself. It's a bit creepy alone out here with all of this open space. I feel exposed and vulnerable. Will I ever get used to open spaces after being banished to a room for most of my adult life? I'm not really sure, but right now is not the time to worry about that. Hurry, hurry, hurry, I kept telling myself as I am now at a jogging pace. All the sudden I have this fear that James is near. I finally reached the cottage and turned the key. Whew! I'm in as I locked the door behind me.

I just stood there for a moment while I let my heart get back to a normal beat. It felt as though it was ready to burst in my chest. I don't think it's healthy to keep having these little bursts of panic. I really need to work on that! Yep, I need to see a shrink!

I put my bag down and took my lunch bag to the fridge. I made a cup of hot tea and went to turn on my bath water. I turned to come out of the bathroom, and there I just stood frozen as James said hello.

"Welcome back from the dead," he said. "Aren't you happy to see your husband?"

I couldn't speak. Fear has taken over and I have lost control of my body. I can't move. I can't speak. Total paralysis.

"Oh honey," he said, "I expected a warmer greeting from you," as he grabbed my hair and pulled me to the ground. He began to rip my shirt, and I knew what was getting ready to happen. I looked around praying someone was going to save me. But in my heart, I knew this would be the end of my life if he has his way.

"Please," I said faintly as I found my voice.

"Please what?" he said. "I'm here to take you home. You know what happens when you try to run from me." He hit me across the face as he was sitting on top of me ripping my clothes from my body. Words spewing from his mouth. "You whore, I heard you have a new man. But not to worry, I'll take care of the both of them and you'll be lucky enough to watch. But not until he sees me take you like a husband takes a wife. Did you really think you could get away that easy?" He punched me across my face several times. "When I'm done with you, no one will want you, bitch."

I'm crying hysterically by now.

He said, "Cry and scream all you want, there's no one to save you this time."

Just then I heard the door fly open and hit the wall with a loud thud. There was Mama with her shotgun pointed right at James. "Get up," she ordered.

He stood and said, "I'm here to get my wife."

"The wife you hired someone to kill? Doesn't seem like a very good husband to me," Mama snarled in a voice I didn't quite recognize. "So go on and get out of here before I shoot you."

"You sure about that, old lady?" he replied. "Can you even see good enough to hit me?" he said as he started backing out the door. His mouth kept running. "You know I'll keep coming for her. I own that bitch," he said.

Just then I swear there was a fire in Mama's eyes, and she fired a shot straight to his heart and down he went. She looked at me and said, "He was never gonna leave this family alone. I can't have that. We've got a mess to clean. If you're okay, go back to the cabin and get Pops."

"I'm fine," I told her. She handed me the shotgun and told me to hurry. I stepped over James's dead body and ran to the cabin like Mama told me.

I had a million things running through my mind. I can't let Mama go to prison for protecting me. Oh god, what's going to happen? I wasn't quite to the cabin when Mike and Mac came running towards me.

"Are you okay? Oh my god, what did he do to you?"

"I'm going to be okay. Mama killed James. He was in the cottage when I got there today. I don't know how he got in. Mama saved my life today." I was shaking beyond my control.

Mike told Mac to get to the cottage to see if Mama is okay. Then he said to Mac, "Let me get her to the cabin and then I'll meet you there at the cottage."

Mac took off to the cottage. I can tell he's still in pain. He was holding his side as he was running. Mike was helping to hold me up as we walked to the cabin. My legs felt like rubber, like they could collapse at any time. We got to the cabin, and everyone came rushing to me. Mike said, "Take care of her. I'm going back for Mac and Mama. Lock the doors and have the guns ready. I don't know how many of James's men are here." I saw him draw his gun as he headed out. Oh god, please let all of them be safe.

Chapter 14

"Mama, Mac are you in here?" he said as he stepped over James's body. They both came walking out of the bathroom.

"The bath water was still running, and the floor is flooded," Mac said. "We were trying to clean up some of the water. I called the sheriff," Mac told them. "They'll be here soon," he said. Mac continued speaking. "They'll want to talk to her. I hope she's up for it."

"She's stronger than you think she is," Mama said. I see it. I see her getting stronger every day. And now with that piece of shit out of the picture, she can get on with her life. How did you boys know he was coming for her today?"

"On the way out, we passed a black SUV with blacked-out windows. The kind James and his men drive. It just didn't sit well so we turned around and then followed from afar. We had to make sure he didn't make us. We drove without lights and stayed at a pretty lengthy distance. I knew it was him. My gut told me it was him," Mac said. "So we followed our instincts and thank God. But, Mama… how did you know?"

"A gut feeling like you, I guess. I was actually gonna just go stay at the cottage with her, but I had seen a man creeping around so I knew I had to find her first. Unfortunately, he got in before I could get here. His smart mouth got him shot!"

"Mama, you know you can't say that to the sheriff, right?"

"Right, but between us, that's why. And he did a number on Jenna's face.

I knew he would never leave her alone. I saw the evil in him when he spoke. I don't believe God will punish me for taking the life of such a horrible man."

"Let's hope you're right, Mama," Mike said.

The sheriff arrived and took statements from everyone involved. He said as far as he could tell, it was self-defense. An open and shut case. I was so relieved.

"But unfortunately, this isn't the end," I told the sheriff. "They'll still come for me. James's men or worse, my son."

"We're not going to let that happen," Mike said. "We'll stay here tonight, and in the morning we'll work on the plan to move you and my family. We need to figure out how James found us. This house should have never even been on the radar. The only other person who knew where we were was the captain. It has to be him."

"I agree," Mac said. "If he knows Jenna is still alive and James is dead, he'll go into hiding. I think we can assume he's being paid well so he'll have enough money to run to a country with no extradition. We'll have to act fast. The problem is who to trust. How many of our law enforcement's members are on James's payroll?"

Mike shrugged his shoulders in response. He then added, "We have to go dark. Right now, all we have is each other. There is no one we can trust at this time."

"Dark it is," Mac replied in agreement. "Let's head back to the cabin."

Well, everyone seemed to be back to normal. Laughing, eating and carrying on like nothing happened. Am I the only person who is shaken by today's events? Mama doesn't even seem rattled about taking the life of another human. I guess he doesn't really count as being human, but still I don't know if I could hold it together after shooting him. I do feel somewhat relieved now that James is dead, but I just want all of this to be over. The days without grief, drama or fear are far too few. I need peace and harmony. I need to be and feel normal. I need to have a day without tears. Seriously! I don't want to cry any more. I've become the Grim Weeper.

For tonight, I think we're all safe, but retaliation is going to happen, I was thinking to myself. The question is when and where. None of them know Lola like I do. She's not one to step aside and she'll kill to get what she wants without a doubt. She already tried to have my life taken but was unsuccessful. She obviously knows about my relationship with Mike and Mac. She'll come for them first and then me. They're trying to keep the shooting out of the news, but I'm planning for the worst. Lola will know about James soon if she doesn't already. More sleepless nights ahead for me. Are we all just sitting ducks waiting on the storm? I hope Mike and Mac have a plan or at least some idea of what's going to ensue.

I don't know if I'll ever be able to go back to the cottage. With my luck, James's ghost will linger just to haunt me. I'm sad about this because the cottage was so perfect. Maybe in time, I can make myself go there again. Mama said a clean-up crew was coming in the next day or two to take care of it. The beautifully preserved green rug was ruined, stained by the blood of an evil man. I'm glad he's gone. I don't have any tears for that man and hope he rots in hell.

I've made a lot of promises to myself as of late, and now I'm going to make one more. I won't let Lola or her drug lord dad hurt anyone in this family… my family. If there's going to be a war, I'm ready for battle. Nothing makes a woman feel more powerful than the need to protect her family. I will protect my family. No matter what.

Just then, Mike came to the door. "Hey, you doing okay?"

"I am, are you?"

"Yeah, I'm good. We're all good. Definitely an eventful day. Do you want to go sit by the fire? Everyone is out there, and Pops asked where you were."

"That's so sweet. I just needed a few minutes to process everything. These last few weeks have been a bit livelier than I'm accustomed to." I gave him a half-hearted smile.

He sat down beside me and held me. "Jenna, I know this all seems like it's never going to end, but I promise you, it will. It's like a game of chess. Now that the king has fallen, so will the rest of them. Just hang in there a little longer and trust the process. I can't promise you that there won't be any more danger, but I can promise to keep you safe. The FBI and DEA are dangerous jobs and we hunt down dangerous people, but Mac and I knew what we signed up for. In due time, justice will prevail. We'll get our happy ending." He kissed me on the forehead and said, "Let's join the family." I nodded in agreement.

We walked to the great room, and sure enough the family was all gathered and multiple conversations were taking place. There was laughter. Mac was playing checkers with Pops, and Mama was just sitting back, watching with what was obviously a very happy heart. How proud they must be of the life they created together and even more so of the family that sits before them. I felt proud just being there with them.

Mike and I took a seat on the round double chair. He grabbed a blanket from the basket sitting near the hearth. It was warm and smelled of the hickory wood burning before us. Mike pulled me in close to him, and before I knew it, we had both fallen asleep. I think exhaustion had set in for all of us.

I woke up at some point and looked around. The entire family was sleeping by the fire. I just smiled and curled back up to Mike. I hope there will be many more nights such as this.

Chapter 15

Iwoke to lots of clatter, loud excited voices and the smell of bacon cooking. I felt confused at first but then realized this is a normal morning for all of them when they gather. I could see Mike and Mac at the table discussing the game plan for moving the family to a new location and Mama was cooking. Sonja, Kristy and her girls were in the kitchen helping. Oh my, I can't believe I slept that long. I guess I need to get to the kitchen and do my part.

"Good morning," I said to everyone as I entered the kitchen. Lots of good morning wishes back to me and then everyone resumed what they were doing. I walked over to Mike and gave him a kiss on the cheek, grabbed a cup of coffee and then went to ask Mama what I could do to help.

"You can help Kristy peel potatoes, otherwise we'll be eating breakfast at lunchtime."

"I heard that, Mama," Kristy said with a smile.

"Good," Mama replied. "Maybe you can focus instead of gossiping. We need to feed these boys. They have a lot to do before we pack up to leave the cabin."

"Has there been a decision made on where we're going yet?" I asked.

Mac replied, "We're trying to get another safe house, but since we have some internal problems, we're bringing in a buddy of mine who also works for the DEA but in a whole different capacity. He's part of an elite team that does some serious top secret shit. I'm waiting on a call back."

"I thought you didn't have a phone and that you two were going to do this on your own. I'm sorry, but I'm having some trust issues right now. I'm surprised you two are not having them too."

"Mac and I have burner phones. They can't be traced," Mike said.

"And there is not a chance that Jimmy would be in on any of this," Mac interjected. "Jimmy served with me. He's also a former seal and we've been close friends for years. In fact, if Mike is ever not around, he's who I would call. We can definitely trust him. He's one of the good guys, and I wish we would have included him sooner."

Right then his phone rang. "Hey," Mac said back to him. Lots of "yeah man", "uh-huh", and "sounds good." Then they hung up. "Mike, you got a minute to speak in private?"

"Yep." Out to the front porch they went. The whole family was still inside, but they were all gathered right on the other side of the door desperately trying to hear what was being said but to no avail. Then they all ran back to the kitchen to pretend like they weren't up to no good. It was a little bit funny to watch grown people behave this way. Including Mama and Pops. Now that's funny!

"Well, we have a plan," Mike announced, then smiled when he realized what just happened. Everyone just started laughing because they knew they were caught eavesdropping. "Jimmy and a few of his men are going to be here in a few hours to help facilitate our move to an undisclosed location. They're bringing two helicopters. Pack what you have to, nothing unnecessary. We will be taking all of our food and cleaning supplies from the cabin. Let's have breakfast and then get busy."

We were back to silence during breakfast. I guess this plan has everyone a bit worried, including me. I always go back to feeling guilty about the situation this family is dealing with. All I can do is hope this plan works out. I can't even imagine what chaos lies ahead. I know I was only at the beach for a brief moment of my life, but right now it's all I can think about. How can I possibly miss something that I barely got to experience? But I really do. Weird.

After breakfast everyone got busy. Much like the day they all arrived. Bags being tossed, food and supplies being boxed, coolers filled with food and drinks, and then there were weapons. Weapons, I can't believe they have this many. I'm guessing my assessment of a war to come was correct. I'm relieved they are prepared but scared of losing any of them. Some days I feel like I should just give myself up to Lola and her dad to protect them, and then I see Mike and a glimpse of what my life can be someday. Maybe I'm being selfish for making all of them leave their homes and go into hiding to protect me. If I surrender maybe their lives can get back to normal. Or will it? The truth is, Lola will probably still come for them to punish me. I don't think there is a win here in any scenario. The war will need to be fought.

I could hear the helicopters approaching. Mac started to direct everyone to the back of the cabin. I took one last look at the cabin and realized none of us will most likely be returning to this magnificent home anytime soon. They'll only have their memories for now. Mama was thinking the exact same thing. I could tell by the sadness in her eyes as she clutched some old framed photos. I went to walk with her hoping to comfort her somehow. She just held my hand and said, "We can make a new home anywhere, we only need to have each other." She always has such beautiful words of comfort, even in the darkest hours.

After the initial confusion and mayhem, we were all finally loaded in the two helicopters. Mac in one with Sonja, Kristy, Mark Ava and Ana and a crew of four men. I was in the second helicopter with Mike, Mama, Pops and a crew of four additional men. I don't know where we're heading, how long we'll be gone or how they managed to pull this off so quickly.

We were in the air and could see the cabin in the distance. Sadness and grief came across Mama and Pops's faces, and the tears began to roll. It was more than I could bear. How could I have let this happen to their family? I was in full blown hysteria. Ranting hysterically about James, telling them we'll never be safe and I don't even know what else. Mike was trying to comfort his parents before my break down. A second later, I felt a sharp prick to my arm. Then I was down.

"What the hell did you do that for?" Mike asked.

"Look," Jimmy said. "You asked me and my men to help you. This is me helping you. She was freaking out, and I can't have everybody falling to pieces while we're flying. It's not safe. She's been through a lot and so have the rest of you. We have a long flight ahead of us, and trust me, you'll thank me later." Mama was just sobbing as Pops was holding her. Jimmy looked around to everyone and then said, "Relax, get some rest. We'll be there in a few hours." No one spoke. Silence took over.

CHAPTER 16

The helicopters landed. I could hear Mike's voice: "Hey, baby, we're landing. Are you awake?" he asked.

But I couldn't focus. Something is wrong, I can't move my body. I was struggling to stay awake. I felt Mike pick me up, and back to sleep I went.

"What did you give her?" Mike asked Jimmy.

"I gave her benzodiazepine. It will wear off in a little while. She'll be fine."

"Don't you ever do that again or I promise I'll beat your ass. I don't care if you are my brother's friend. That was not cool." Both men grumbled and went on their way.

I woke several hours later in a small room. The house was quiet, and bags were everywhere, inside and out. We had landed and I slept through it all. I remembered the prick to my arm and suddenly I was pissed. I was drugged against my will. I immediately went to look for Mike. When I finally found him, he was talking to Mac and a few other guys including Jimmy. "You asshole," I blurted out. "Was this your idea? I don't appreciate being drugged without my consent." I was talking to Mike, and suddenly they all looked afraid.

"Jenna, I swear, I didn't know," Mike replied.

Right then Jimmy stepped in and said, "It wasn't Mike, it was me. I made the decision all by myself."

"Why would you do that? You don't even know me."

"Look," he said, "I'm sorry, but you were acting a little out there. I had to make sure we had a safe flight. You're right, I don't know you. All the more reason to assume it could have gotten much worse. I'm a certified paramedic. I promise what I did was legal and in your best interest."

Still pissed, I turned and walked away from all of them. "Such bull," I blurted.

"Jenna!" Mike hollered practically chasing me.

I stopped and turned to him. "What?" I replied in an angry tone.

"Jenna, I'm sorry. I'm not making excuses for what he did, but he believed it was right at the time. Are you okay?"

"I'm fine," I retorted.

"Come with me," he said. "I want to show you something."

Reluctantly I agreed. "What is it you want to show me?" still curt in my tone.

"Let's take a walk, it's not far." We were just a few steps into our walk before I recognized the smell.

I squealed. "We're at the beach."

He looked at me puzzled. "How did you know?"

"The smell. I will never forget the salty smell of the ocean. It only took once to fall in love with the beach. I can't believe we're here."

"It's about a half mile walk from the house to the beach," Mike said. I could tell he was happy that I was happy after the earlier events.

At the end of the trail, the beach emerged in all its glory. I could see the rest of the family playing in the waves, except for Mac.

"This beach looks different," I said. The water is unbelievable, boasting beautiful hues of aqua and turquoise. Nothing like the beach in South Carolina. "Where are we?"

"We're on a private island in the Bahamas," Mike stated matter-of-factly. "The house is small in comparison to our cabin, but it will have to do for now," he said with a laugh. He walked me down to the rest of the family and then told me he had to get back to business for a little while. He kissed me softly on my lips and then handed me my seashell bag from his pocket. I was tickled. Ava and Ana wanted to look for seashells with me.

What seemed like hours later, Mike and Mac joined us along with a few men from the crew. I was so happy to see they brought sandwiches. I was starving. My clothes were soaked, and I was covered in sand. Mike laughed and asked me why I am the only person in this condition.

"I've got nothing," I replied with a very big smile. "I'm ready for that sandwich now." We all sat to eat our sandwiches while enjoying the warm rays of sunshine and the beautiful view directly in front of us.

Not long after we finished eating, Mac announced we needed to get unpacked before it gets dark. "The crew will keep watch around the clock, but after dark, it becomes more difficult." After several snarky remarks and some minor complaints, everyone exited the beach at a turtle's pace. I wasn't sure if it was exhaustion or their unhappiness about having to leave to unpack. I'm going to go with the latter, I thought to myself.

After getting back to the house, everyone seemed to be looking for a space to call their own. But Mike was right. This house was really small for this many people. One of the rooms had four bunks with small drawers for each. Kristy and her family took that room. Mama and Pops took the room at the end of the hall. Mike and I as well as Mac and Sonja basically had a room that housed a full bed, a tiny closet and a nightstand with four drawers. The flight crew took the sunroom. All these people sharing two bathrooms. This should be interesting, I was thinking.

Just then Ava blurted, "I think we need a boys' bathroom and girls' bathroom." Mama quickly agreed stating the girls will take the one with a bathtub. Boys get the one with a shower stall. Everyone was in agreement. I already loved the idea, and I was thrilled Mama voiced her opinion. I knew what Mama said would be the law of the land. I was simply happy to not be sharing a bathroom with men we don't know. I was amused by all of this.

By the time everyone was settled, it was late. After midnight, I think. We all showered which took a while and were asleep by 2:30 A.M. I'm guessing. I didn't hear any chatter anyway. All that is except me. I was awake thinking about the last month. First preparing for my escape to now living it. This seems like a story no one would ever believe. This could almost be a fairy tale, except it's really scary if you know the villainous characters, but it's also a love story: A victim meets her Prince Charming, a real story of family survival. Who would ever believe such a story. I hope when this is all over, I'm alive to tell it to my grandchildren. I want to tell it to other women survivors in similar circumstances to hopefully give them a chance to live their own fairytale. I want to use the money Mac gave me to open a shelter for abused women. It's decided. I have a plan. I smiled and felt a rush of happiness come over me. Now I can sleep.

<h1 style="text-align:center">CHAPTER 17</h1>

I was abruptly awakened by something licking my face. I was startled and then instantly happy when I saw what it was. The most adorable tiny blond puppy.

Mike said, "Isn't he cute? Want to keep him?"

"Yes! I would love to keep him, but where did you find a puppy on a private island?"

"Actually there were six puppies," he said. "A few of the crew are looking for the mama. It's possible someone brought them here by boat and dumped them. We just don't know. Jimmy found them on his watch last night on the other side of the island. Hopefully we found all of them. Everyone is up and looking, except Mama; she's cooking breakfast. Your favorite, pancakes and bacon."

"Yum," I said. "Such excitement so early. It's going to be a great day," I said picking up my puppy. Oh my goodness, he's cute. I threw some clothes on and pulled my hair up. Grabbed my toothbrush and toothpaste in one hand and my puppy in the other and headed to the girls' bathroom to brush my teeth. But someone else was in there so I stood waiting. I'm guessing this will be a process. Just then the door opened and Sonja came out smelling freshly showered.

"Good morning," she said and then ruffled my puppy's head. "They're all so cute," she said.

"Oh, I can't wait to see the rest of them," I replied and shut the bathroom door behind me remembering to lock it. I freshened up, brushed my teeth and headed outside. This seemed to be where all the excitement is coming from.

Once outside, I put the puppy down so he could potty. Then I scooped him up and joined the others. Apparently, they found the mama dog but she's not doing well. They don't think she's going to make it. She has a deep infected wound on her side and is too sick to nurse her babies. "I'm going to get Mama. I'm sure she has some old remedies that could work for this poor thing. I'll be right back."

I ran back in the house and told Mama about the injured dog. She turned off the stove and grabbed her first aid kit and came back with me.

She looked at the dog and said, "I don't think we can save her. She needs surgery, but she's already so weak. And we don't have antibiotics. I can give her something to make her sleep and she won't wake up." Tears were already forming in my eyes. Ava and Ana were crying too. I was so sad for her and her puppies. Mama gave her a shot, and she slipped peacefully to sleep.

Mike came over to me and hugged me. He said, "I'll bury her," and picked her up. He walked towards the beach path alone. I just couldn't go with him.

Mama said, "Let's have breakfast and figure out how we're going to take care of the other seven.

"Wait, I thought there were only six," I said.

"They found another one close to the mama," Kristy said. "They look to be about two weeks old. We'll have to figure out what to feed them and come up with a feeding schedule."

Everyone was now gathered in the kitchen eating breakfast with full-on conversations taking place about the puppies. Still sad about the mama dog, I realized she was no longer suffering. It's hard to say when the injury took place or even how she was injured. I'm just thankful the rest of the puppies are safe. Although I'm still baffled about how the dogs got here in the first place. Maybe she was brought here before the puppies were born.

It was decided at some point that Jimmy and one of his men would make a trip back to the mainland for additional supplies for all of us to include baby formula and bottles for the puppies. Mama said some instant baby rice would be good too. So they left and said it would be late before they got back.

Several hours passed, and they were all crying and whimpering. I'm certain they are hungry. "I can't *not* feed them," I announced to everyone. "This many crying puppies is breaking my heart." I got up and went to the kitchen still holding my crying puppy. "There has to be something we can feed them." I found a box of instant cream of wheat and mixed a couple of packages with warm milk. I made it thin and fed mine first with a plastic teaspoon. He finally figured out that it was food which made the process easier. Then Mama, Kristy and Sonja each picked one up to start feeding them. Mike just watched me in amazement.

Mama said, "You're going to be a great mama someday." I thanked her. I'm sure she remembered I was already a mama once upon a time. My thoughts wandered briefly to my son before I was distracted when Mike handed me another puppy. This one picked up the feeding process much faster than my puppy. After they were all fed, I went to get my duffle bag. I opened it up and put several towels and a blanket inside and then put the puppies in it. In no time they were sleeping, all cuddled together in a puppy pile. Such a rewarding afternoon, I thought.

I must have dozed off. I woke to whimpering puppies. I'm guessing it's feeding time again. Oh boy, we're going to be busy. I picked up the duffle with the puppies and carried them outside to potty. One by one they did their business and then I went to the kitchen to make another batch of instant cream of wheat. The others must have heard me and came to help. We chatted about names. I announced that I named mine Dune since he was found on the beach. Everyone loved it and were trying to come up with names for the others. We were also trying to figure out what kind of dogs they were. The mama dog looked like a small Labrador retriever mix, maybe fifty pounds. But who knows what the daddy was. I guess it really doesn't matter, they're cute and they've all been claimed so I know they'll have loving homes. Kristy let each of the girls pick one, I'm taking one, Mama and Pops are taking one, Sonja is taking one and two were taken by Jimmy's crew. Such a relief.

It was almost 9 P.M. when the helicopter landed. Everyone rushed outside to assist with unloading supplies, except me. I stayed with the puppies. We're trying to keep them together for now to help keep them warm. Sonja volunteered to take tonight with them since I had them most of the day. I'm relieved to have a break, but then I'm worried about not being there. Why is everything in life measured by choices? It just complicates things that shouldn't be complicated. Maybe it's just me?

Anyway, after we put everything away…again…I used the baby formula and a little bit of cream of wheat to make fourteen bottles, two for each to get through the night. Oh my, that's a lot of bottles, I thought. Anyway, it was much easier and faster to feed them with bottles. Mac said he would help Sonja with the feedings tonight so I felt okay leaving the task to her. Just then I realized I was acting as if they're all mine and sort of took charge. For some reason I feel obligated to care for them since they no longer have a mama. Maybe it stems from my own needs for not having a mama or maybe from not getting to be the mama to Junior like I should have been. Who knows, but it feels so good to be needed.

Later in the evening, I finally got my turn in the bathroom and I took a really long hot shower. Goodness, I feel so much better. I used my lavender body wash and lotion. I felt clean, relaxed and ready for a good night's sleep. My hair was still wet so I knew I would be looking crazy in the morning, but I didn't care. I wanted sleep, glorious beautiful sleep. I crawled into bed only to find Mike waiting for me. Judging by his woody, sleep will have to wait.

CHAPTER 18

Ilooked at the clock and panic set in. Oh my goodness, it's 9:30 A.M. The
puppies! Mike was already up and gone. The house was quiet. I looked everywhere and no humans, no puppies. I went out front and Mike was sitting
on the porch drinking his coffee.

"Good morning," I said. "Where is everyone? Where are the puppies?"

"Everyone is at the beach, including the puppies. No worries, Mama and
Sonja fed them before going to the beach. Mama thought they could use some
exercise. After a few regular feedings, it seems they are feeling energetic.
They're apparently making everyone tired so the plan is to wear them out so
they'll sleep better tonight."

I laughed. I hope it works. I'll change, grab some coffee and then we can
go to the beach too."

"Sounds good. I'll be right here waiting for you," he said.

I changed into my swimsuit, grabbed my seashell bag and a cup of coffee
and met Mike on the porch.

"Thank you for last night," he said. "I love making love to you." I blushed
and told him it was pretty perfect for me too. We held hands as we headed to
the beach.

"I can't wait to see Dune," I told him.

"Me either," he replied. We started walking faster and faster until he let
go of my hand and started to race me. The kid in me couldn't resist the chal-
lenge. I bolted and caught up to him, but unfortunately I was wearing half of

my coffee when we got there. We were out of breath from running and laughing. Everyone stopped to see what the fuss was all about.

Mike said, "What is everyone looking at? I won the race. I'm faster than her." He laughed at himself and then everyone else laughed too, including me even though I don't agree he won the race.

"If I weren't in such a hurry to see my puppy, I'd go for a redo," I said walking directly past him and over to the puppies. I scooped up Dune and gave him a big kiss. I'm guessing by the wag of his tail, he's happy to see me too.

Dune fell asleep on my chest so I laid out my towel to sunbathe while I cuddled him. He didn't seem to mind the heat and neither did I. I could see Mike and Mac chatting a short distance from the others and then Mac took a call. I instantly felt that worried, sick feeling I sometimes get when they get a call. Something is going on. I can feel it.

Not long later, Mike walked over to me. He said, "We've got business to take care of. We're leaving to go back to the bureau. There are some new leads on Lola and her dad."

"Ugh," I said. "I was hoping I didn't have to hear those names for a little while."

"They bought tickets to fly out of the US tomorrow. It's now or never. We have to do this. You'll be safe here. Jimmy and five of his guys are staying here on the island to keep watch over you and the family. Hopefully we're going to apprehend the both of them." He turned to leave but then came back and sat beside me. Oh no, I was thinking. And then here it came.

"Jenna, I have some bad news. I was going to wait to tell you when I got back, but it just doesn't feel right. There's no easy way to tell you so I'm just going to say it. Junior was killed during his apprehension attempt this morning. They raided James's mansion in the wee hours of the morning, and Junior came out shooting. All guns were on him; he took seventeen bullets. I'm so sorry. I promise the intent was to capture, but it just didn't go as planned. The drugs were seized in the process. I didn't tell you about the raid because I didn't want you to be worried."

I abruptly sat up almost dropping Dune. I began to cry. That familiar ache in my heart was front and center. This time the realization of never seeing my son again became as real as real can get. I knew in that moment I would feel guilty for the rest of my life for betraying him and now I'll never have a chance to make things right with him. I can't breathe. I got up, handed Dune to Mike and started running. I didn't know to where, only that I had to get away. Far away. I should have endured my life with James to protect my son. Isn't that what a good mother would do?

I ran until I could no longer run and then I fell to my knees crying hysterically. My baby is gone. Even though I could only love him from afar, I still loved him with all my heart. I was his mother. I cried until I could cry no more, and like every other time, I picked myself up and started walking back. I don't even know how much time had passed, but the sun was starting to set.

I could see Mama walking towards me in the distance. I'm not sure her words of wisdom are what I need or want right now. As we got closer to each other, she held her arms out to me and I just fell into her arms. We cried together briefly without saying a word. Then she took my hand, and we walked the rest of the way back. She must have sensed my thoughts because no words were spoken. Once we were at the house, I showered and went to bed. Mike obviously had to leave, and I was glad. I needed time to process and grieve the loss of my only child.

It was a long night. My thoughts were all over the place. From blaming myself to blaming James and then to blaming Mac and Mike. If they had just stayed out of it, I would still be in my room and Junior would be alive. But by morning, my logical side accepted what my heart already knew. That Junior was undeniably just like his father. He was headed for no good, and what happened to him was inevitable. With his lack of experience in his father's world of business, it was just matter of time. Unfortunately, his time was short. My heart will never be the same. I lost part of me today.

Chapter 19

It was nearly noon the next day when Mama knocked on my door. "Can I come in?" she asked.

"The door is open," I replied. I sat up in bed to greet her, my hair a mess and my eyes so swollen from crying that I could barely see.

Mama handed Dune to me. "Someone is missing you," she said. "He's been whimpering and hasn't taken a bottle in over twelve hours." She handed me his bottle so I could try. He instantly latched on. I wrapped him in my blanket while I fed him. Mama just watched. When he was done, she said, "I'll take him if you like, but I think it best if you come out of this room and let me fix you something to eat. Come join your family. It's usually the best medicine for a grieving heart." I nodded to let her know I would be out shortly. I grabbed my clothes and toiletries and proceeded to the shower. Maybe I'll feel human again after washing.

I did feel somewhat better. I headed to the kitchen where Mama and the rest of the family were waiting. She made me an egg and cheese sandwich with a fruit cup on the side. Apparently I was starving because I inhaled it. Mama made me another, and I almost finished that too. But then that made sense. I realized I hadn't eaten since the night before last. I was surprised to learn that no one had eaten breakfast this morning because they all waited on me to get up. How can this family be so perfect? Really, I mean it. All of them. I love them. I turned to look at them and then I spoke. "No words can express my gratitude to all of you. Thank you for taking me in as part of your family and for being there for me."

I was waiting on the awkward moment of silence, but they unilaterally said, "We love you too" and continued eating.

Right then Kristy said, "That can change if you make us wait this long to eat breakfast again." Everyone laughed.

I smiled back at her and said, "I'll set an alarm next time."

After brunch I volunteered to do the dishes. I wanted to be alone for just a bit. Everyone else had already headed to the beach. I told them I would be there shortly, but I'm not sure that I'll be very pleasant to be around. I feel like a Debbie downer. It seems as though sadness and chaos follow me. I don't want that anymore. I want to be normal. I can't help but wonder if normal will ever exist in my world. Every day I just keep chugging along. There are such beautiful moments and then the next disaster presents itself. Is this life for everyone or just me?

I finished the dishes and then went to put my swimsuit on. On my way out, I checked on the puppies. They were all sleeping soundly. Mama fed them and took them out for a potty break so they should be good for a few hours anyway.

I took my time walking to the beach. It felt good to just breathe in this amazing salty air. My mood instantly lifted. Eventually, I know my heart will heal. Maybe not anytime soon and I know that no one ever really recovers from the loss of a child. However, time will help with acceptance. My existence will be different without him, but the few really great memories will hopefully always carry me through the tough times ahead. Just then I turned the corner and could see them all sitting in a group just talking and laughing. In that moment, I knew my life will go on. I'm going to be okay. Somehow, I felt comforted by my own thoughts.

I joined the group but passed on sea shelling with Ava and Ana. "I'm just going to sit here today if that's okay." They seemed to understand that I needed to be alone and went on their way. I sat quietly in my beach chair just watching the waves lapping on the shoreline. Small birds running close to the water and then running back when the next wave approached. They seemed to be enjoying the game. The sights and sounds were so relaxing. If only life could be so simple, I thought. I wish Mike could be here with me right now. I really miss him. I miss his smell, his touch, but mostly I miss his beautiful laugh. Please don't be gone too long, I was thinking to myself.

About two hours passed, and Sonja asked me to go back to the house with her to get the puppies. Of course, I agreed. We made small talk on the way back. Apparently one of the guards was following close behind us because he joined in on our conversation. Sonja told him that he didn't really need to stay with us and that we'd be fine.

He was quick to say, "No way, ma'am, our orders are to escort you ladies everywhere." We both just nodded in agreement and went on about our business. We did learn that his name is Tyler and that he has the night shift tonight. He seemed like a kid. No more than nineteen or twenty, I would say. I guess it's good having the guards here. It does make me feel so much safer, even if they are young. I can't help but wonder if these young lads knew what they were signing up for. I mean, James was a ruthless character and would have stopped at nothing to get his way. Even if it meant taking someone's life. It's sad that we live in a world where we have to hide from bad people.

We went to get the puppies, but they were awake and crawling out of the duffle bag. "Oh no," I said as I started counting to make sure they were all here. Luckily they were. "We'd better get to figuring out a kennel of sorts," I said. This sure didn't last long. We scooped them back in the duffle and took them to the kitchen to make bottles. They were all crying. We couldn't feed them fast enough. Then back outside for another potty break.

"I'm so thankful we're all sharing puppy duty. This is exhausting," Sonja said laughing.

"It sure is," I agreed. "I think Kristy and the girls have tonight and tomorrow so we get to sleep in. That's the plan anyway. I'm definitely looking forward to a quiet night," I stated. Sonja nodded in agreement.

We finished tending to the puppies and then I headed to the shower. Sonja headed back to the beach. I sure am missing my lavender bubble bath from the cottage. It just doesn't seem right to lallygag in the bathroom with so many of us trying to share the same space. Someday I hope to have a big bathtub all to myself. For now a shower will do. However, after my shower, I think I'll cook dinner for everyone. They have all done so much for me. Not only do I want to make them dinner, it's also the right thing to do. I think I'll make a shrimp boil. The shrimp is fresh so it should be perfect. I'm getting hungry just thinking about it. Note to self… take a fast shower.

After I showered and dressed, I headed to the kitchen. I got out the biggest pot I could find. I added red skin baby potatoes to the pot and let them simmer for a bit.f Next I added the smoked sausage cut in slices, and the corn on the cob. I let that cook for about ten minutes. Lastly, I added the shrimp, Old Bay seasoning, garlic salt, pepper and parsley and a stick of butter. I sliced a fresh baguette to serve with it. Just then, they all started coming in from the beach.

"It smells yummy in here," Mama stated.

"Whatever you're cooking, I hope it's ready soon. I'm starving," Pops said. Lots of nods and yums from the others too.

"I made shrimp boil," I announced. "I hope it turned out okay, this is my first time making it. It's ready whenever everyone wants to eat."

"Mama said, "Wash hands please. I'll help you get all this to the table after I wash my own hands." While the crew washed hands, I set the table. I was feeling pretty proud of myself. It really does look and smell delicious. I wish Mike and Mac were here to enjoy it with us.

Everyone gathered in the tiny kitchen, and just like always, plates were being passed, food was flying, and lots of different conversations. Beautiful chaos is all I could think. My dinner choice was a big hit after a day on the beach. I needed a distraction from my sadness, and this right here is exactly what I needed. Once everyone was done, I washed the dishes.

After I finished cleaning up, I gave a quick nod good night to everyone and headed to my room. I took two Tylenol pm's to hopefully help me sleep. I don't want another night like last night; my heart just can't endure.

Lucky for me, sleep came fast.

Chapter 20

I awoke feeling rested, but my thoughts were only about my son this morning. It took all I had to fight back the tears. Thank goodness for the puppies. They are a welcomed distraction. My little guy came bouncing. He was so happy to see me. After discussing over breakfast, we're going to each take care of our own puppies today and see if it's any less exhausting. I made the formula mix in a very large pitcher to accommodate four to five feedings per puppy. Each person can pour what they need when they need it. I decided I'm going to put Dune in my bed with me tonight too. Hopefully I don't squash him. He's still so tiny. Maybe I'll give it a trial run with him and take a nap. I've just been so tired lately. That fast my thoughts are back to Mike and Mac. I really wish one or both would check in, or better yet come home. This is the third day and still no word from them. I hope everything is going okay.

I was playing with Dune in my room and heard some commotion coming from the kitchen. The guards had their guns drawn and told me to go to the furthest room in the house, which would be Mama's room. I turned to go as directed but not before I asked what is going on. I was informed that we had intruders on the island. Oh no, not again I thought. My mood quickly changed from sadness to fear. I'm wondering if James's men had found me. It now appears that everyone, not just me, is being directed to the furthest room in the house.

Once we were all in the room, the chatter and speculation were nonstop. Except me. I sat frozen not saying a word. I just kept praying that the intruders were not from James's crew. About thirty minutes had passed, and we could still hear conversation outside. Next thing I knew, Tyler came to the door to tell us everything was okay and we could exit the room. We were all relieved of worry. Mama asked Tyler who the intruders were.

He quickly replied, "Some kids on their boat out for a joyride. They thought they would check the island out. I told them this was a private island and they had to go. None of them bothered to ask questions when we all came out with guns pointed at them. They gladly went on their way." He chuckled as he was delivering the news. He seemed to be entertained and amused by the whole situation. Maybe because these kids were no older than himself and he could probably relate to their curiosity about the island.

"I'm just happy that things went smoothly and that it didn't have anything to do with James or his business," I said.

Everyone kind of shrugged it off as they returned to their daily activities. It started to rain not long after the excitement ended. I took Dune out for his potty break just in time. Now it's raining really hard. The clouds in the distance look pretty scary.

Pops said, "Let's turn the news on to see what this weather is gonna do. Hopefully, there's no hurricanes heading this way."

I just looked at him and he smiled. "Hurricanes?" I asked. "Really?"

"Well, we are on an island surrounded by water," Pops said. Now he had the attention of everyone in the room. We all sort of huddled together to watch the news for updates about the weather. Luckily the news just called it a mild tropical storm so I think we're going to be okay. All the sudden the power went out. Oh good grief.

"Now what?" Mama said.

One of the crew came to check on all of us. "Everyone doing ok?" he asked.

"All good here," Pops replied. "Just tell me this house has a generator."

"It does," one of the crew replied, "but only enough to run the refrigerator and maybe a few lights and the TV. I think it's best we not use all the juice yet just in case the storm picks up. For now just hang tight and stay together as much as possible. The cameras aren't currently working. We'll have to watch the perimeters from outside."

It just feels creepy without lights, I was thinking to myself. Why do I always get a bad feeling? The whole intruder thing and then a storm that causes a power outage in the same day just hours apart feels way wrong. I started to tell Mama my thoughts, when she stood up and grabbed her shotgun. She obviously feels something too.

"Whoa," Pops said. "What's going on with my best girl?"

"Something isn't right," Mama said.

Kristy chimed in with her agreement. "Now what do we do?" she asked.

"If any of you have guns, you need to get them," Mama ordered. Everyone just stood there looking at her.

"Hurry up," I said.

"You stay here," Mama told me. "Ava, Ana, you do the same. The rest of you get back here in a hurry." They scattered off to get their guns while the fear in me took over once more. Mama could see it and told me to snap out of it. I could hear her saying the words, but my body wouldn't move.

And there it was. My fears have been validated. Lola appeared behind Mama. Her words were cold as she looked at me. "You and I have business to discuss. So unless you want me to take this pretty woman's life, I suggest you come with me."

Again, I could only stand there frozen in time.

Mama answered for me. She said, "She's not going anywhere with you. You'll have to kill me first."

"Don't test me, woman. You will die tonight if you don't hand her over right now."

Ava and Ana cowered behind me. That was enough to make me come to my senses. "Okay, Lola, you win," I told her. "I'll come with you, but only if you promise to let my family go."

"Your family," she sneered. "These people aren't your family. You don't have a family. Your son is dead, although we both know he wasn't really your son. He was mine, and you know that's the truth."

Something inside me snapped. I went at her head-on not considering the possibility of being shot. Suddenly, I was not in control of my own actions. I felt like a crazy person. My hands were wrapped tightly around her neck. As I was choking her, I proceeded to tell her that she and James made a monster out of my son. She dropped the gun out of weakness from me choking her, and Kristy quickly picked it up. Mama was telling me to let her go, but I just couldn't. I wanted to hurt her. Maybe even kill her for all the years of pain she and James have caused.

Just then the crew showed up. They had Lola's drug lord dad in custody as well as two of his men. The guards kept telling me to let go of her, but I just couldn't. I knew she would keep coming for me and my family. It was now or never, and right now I'm thinking if I end her life, the outcome will be better for everyone.

Mama chimed in and sternly told me to stop before I killed her. "You don't want to do this," she said. "Let go of her."

I paused for a brief moment before letting go. My hands fell to my side. Mac and Mike walked in apparently just before that. Mike just stared at me for a minute and asked me if I was okay.

"I think am," I replied. "I'm so happy to see you," I said as tears started to build in my eyes.

Lola then started to speak directly to me. She said, "You're right, I will keep coming for you. You ruined my life, my family's life, and our way of life. You will never know peace, I can promise you that."

I looked at her but didn't respond. I knew in my heart she spoke the truth. She will find a way to keep coming for me.

While we were waiting on the Coast Guard to arrive, Mike told me they had eyes and ears on Lola and that's how they knew she had found us on the island. Apparently, James placed a tracking device in my duffle and that's how they kept finding us. They sent the kids on the boat to see how many people were on the island and paid them a couple hundred bucks. Those kids had no idea what they were doing and who they were doing it for.

It all made sense now, I thought. How did I not see it?

"They were on to Bert aka Mac long before we even knew," I said.

"But it's over now," Mike replied as he was hugging me. "They're going to prison for life."

"What about the people that still work for them?" I asked.

"Their loyalty will move on to the next person in charge," he said. "I've been assured if we stay out of their business, they'll stay out of ours. It's a win-win for all of us."

Several agents took statements from everyone and then hauled Lola, her dad and his two men off to prison. They will be held without bail pending trial. Mike said that hopefully, they'll all take a plea, life in prison without the possibility of parole and the death penalty will be off the table. Then there won't be a trial. It will finally be over. Either way, it's bye-bye to their crooked ways. After this case, Mac and I have decided to retire. I'm tired of chasing bad guys. We'll all be placed in the witness protection program just in case they don't hold up their end of the bargain.

The relief I felt in that moment is indescribable. Freedom. I have a new chance at life. I'm going to live it right this time.

Everyone stayed up late discussing today's events, and of course that involved a feast! I was so hungry. Mama made biscuits and gravy for dinner, along with scrambled eggs and fried potatoes.

After dinner, we all fed the pups and then I called it a night for myself.

Mike said, "I'll join you shortly." I was asleep in a matter of seconds, I think. I never heard him come to bed.

CHAPTER 21

I woke up at 6 A.M. feeling sick to my stomach. I ran to the bathroom to throw up. Oh my, that came out of nowhere, I was thinking to myself. Maybe it was from eating so much and so late last night. I'm not sure. But there is nothing worse than throwing up first thing in the morning.

I quickly showered and got dressed. I went back to our room, and Mike asked me if I was okay. I assured him I was.

"Let's go to the beach," I said. "Sonja said there's lots of shells after a storm."

"Ok, sounds good to me, but I need coffee," he said. I laughed and told him I would brew us some while he got dressed.

I went to the kitchen and first brewed Mike's giant cup of coffee and then I started on my own giant cup.

Mama walked in and said, "You probably shouldn't be drinking that. Especially a cup that size," she added. I looked at her confused. She then said, "Caffeine is not good for the baby."

Still confused, I said, "What baby?"

She hugged me and said, "A mama always knows. It's a feeling, and your morning sickness confirmed it. You're going to have a baby. My grandchild and your second chance." Then she hugged me.

"I don't know how Mike is going to feel if what you say turns out to be true. I mean, this isn't something we've even talked about."

"Sweet girl, it's true enough, and Mike will be elated. Trust me," Mama said.

I just looked at her in disbelief.

Mike walked into the kitchen right then and asked, "What will I be elated about?" He saw my tears as I was trying to wipe them away. "Tell me," he said. "What is it?"

"Your mama thinks I'm pregnant with your child," I blurted. He paused as if to process what I just said. I immediately apologized for not being careful if I was in fact pregnant.

He hugged me tight and said, "I hope we are having a baby. That's the best news I've heard in a long time."

"I'm so glad you're not mad," I said.

"Why would I be mad? I told you, I'm in love with you. I knew you were the one the moment I met you at the beach. This is perfect timing too given that I'm retiring. I can help take care of our baby."

By then everyone was up and talking about it. There are apparently no secrets in this family. I shared that I thought maybe they were being a bit to presumptuous. It really could be nothing. Kristy chimed in and said, "If Mama says you're pregnant, you're definitely pregnant. Somehow she just always knows."

"Mama knows lots of things," Sonja said. "You can't slip anything past her. I think she has a second set of eyes and ears somewhere that no one else can see," she said laughing at her own comment. Then I started laughing too.

"I heard that," Mama said from the kitchen.

"See, I told you" Sonja said laughing once more.

Mike announced to everyone that we're going sea-shelling. "Do you want to take Dune with us?" he asked.

"I definitely do," I replied. "We'll see you all in a bit," as he took my hand and led me to the door.

Once we got outside, he said, "I'm glad I finally have you all to myself."

"Well, not exactly," I replied looking at Dune. "You'll have to share me apparently with our dog and our future baby."

"God, I love the sound of that," Mike said. "Our baby. How beautiful is that?"

I looked at him in total admiration. "I love you," Mike. I'm excited for our life together. I hope it's a little less eventful than it has been lately. A little too much excitement for me. I picture us in a small cottage near the beach living a quiet life."

"Sounds perfect," he said, "but with my family, there's always something going on so I wouldn't count on a quiet life."

I smiled at him and said, "You're probably right about that!" We laughed for a minute and then he stopped to kiss me softly on my lips.

My mind drifted off for a minute or two as I pondered over my future. I realized I really do get a second chance. I get the fairy tale. I will no longer live in fear of someday. My someday is here.

The End